"*Human* sacrifices?" Hallie gasped. "You mean, they actually burned *people*?"

Elder Sidlaw nodded.

"And you're still celebrating a feast where things like that were done?"

"Why not?" Elder Sidlaw replied calmly. "It's a tradition."

Hallie and Becky watched as a low platform with a stake in its center was erected in the middle of what would become the bonfire.

"I can't believe what I'm seeing," Hallie said nervously. "This looks like they're getting ready for the real thing."

"It's totally harmless," the elder assured her. "In primitive times a maiden would have been sacrificed to the people's patron Goddess." He hesitated. "Now, of course, a straw dummy represents the maiden."

Becky was staring at the scaffolding, her eyes wide.

"Burned at the stake! What an awful way to die!" she said in a horrified voice. "Even if I believed in some Goddess and all that baloney, I still wouldn't want to die like that."

Don't miss these other terrifying
thrillers by Bebe Faas Rice:

Class Trip
Love You to Death

And look for
The Principal
The Substitute
The Coach
Deadly Stranger
by M. C. Sumner

Baby-sitter's Nightmare
Baby-sitter's Nightmare II
Sweet Dreams
Sweetheart
Teen Idol
Running Scared
by Kate Daniel

CLASS TRIP II

BEBE FAAS RICE

HarperPaperbacks
A Division of HarperCollins*Publishers*

This is a work of fiction. The characters, incidents, and dialogues are products of the author's imagination and are not to be construed as real. Any resemblance to actual events or persons, living or dead, is entirely coincidental.

HarperPaperbacks *A Division of* HarperCollins*Publishers*
10 East 53rd Street, New York, N.Y. 10022

Copyright © 1995 by Daniel Weiss Associates, Inc., and Bebe Faas Rice

Cover art copyright © 1995 Daniel Weiss Associates, Inc.

All rights reserved. No part of this book may be used or reproduced in any manner whatsoever without written permission of the publisher, except in the case of brief quotations embodied in critical articles and reviews. For information address Daniel Weiss Associates, Inc., 33 West 17th Street, New York, New York 10011.

Produced by Daniel Weiss Associates, Inc., 33 West 17th Street, New York, New York 10011.

First printing: January 1995

Printed in the United States of America

HarperPaperbacks and colophon are trademarks of HarperCollins*Publishers*

10 9 8 7 6 5 4 3 2 1

To Duff—My favorite critic and technical adviser. And to Jackie, who told me about bone fires.

ONE
The Place of Worship

In the smoky, wavering light of the torches, the white-robed leader's pale eyes glitter like blue ice.

"The Goddess has turned her face from us," he says accusingly. "It has been ten years since our last sacrifice, and She is angry. Now the crops have failed, and we have had no live births among the women of the village."

A murmur of frightened assent runs over the crowd gathered below. The people raise their faces to him trustfully.

Behind him on a dais sit twelve men also dressed in white robes. They are seated in high-backed, thronelike chairs behind a long black table. Their eyes are fixed on their leader.

1

"The ancient gods are not dead," one says reverently. "They live in fire and water and wood and stone. And The Goddess is mightiest of them all. We must not offend our Goddess."

The other men on the dais nod wisely.

"All reverence to The Goddess!" someone in the crowd calls out.

"All reverence to The Goddess!" the rest repeat.

One of the twelve men turns to the leader and says, "But we have made sacrifices. The animals. The straw burnings. Have they not shown our devotion?"

"No," the leader tells him. "Those were only symbolic sacrifices. Straw maidens and animals no longer satisfy The Goddess and cause her to bring fertility to our fields and to our wives."

He pauses and looks around. "We must have a Fire Maiden for the feast of Beltane," he says in a low, clear voice.

There is a collective gasp, followed by a moment of uneasy silence. A faint wail comes from one of the back rows, but it is quickly suppressed.

"Yes," the leader says. "A Fire Maiden. The Goddess requires it."

The faces of the men at the table are grim and set. In the audience several women have begun to weep.

"Who will choose the Fire Maiden?" someone finally asks.

"The twelve elders and I will make the final decision," replies the leader. "Just as we did last time."

A thin, bitter-faced woman in the crowd stands up and says, "Ten years ago I gave my daughter—my beautiful, flame-haired daughter—to The Goddess. I was proud to do it. Is no one here willing to do the same for the good of our people?"

She glares angrily at the frightened people around her. No one will meet her eyes.

"Well?" she demands.

"Maybe The Goddess will be merciful and send us a sacrifice from The Outside," someone says.

Voices join in hopefully. "Yes, a sacrifice from The Outside."

The bitter-faced woman laughs. "What cowards you all are! Do you think someone from The Outside will wander in here, like a fly to a spiderweb?"

The leader, who has been listening thoughtfully, says, "Someone from The Outside? Yes, why not? We will send out a few of our best men to find the perfect sacrifice and lure her to the village. And then . . ."

TWO

Hallie Anderson hung over the front seat of the ancient white van and tapped the driver's shoulder.

"What's that noise, Adam? That little *ping*—hear it? Is something wrong with the motor?"

Adam French shrugged. "It does that sometimes. Nothing to worry about."

"Nothing to worry about?" Hallie echoed incredulously. "We're in the middle of nowhere, on a mountain road I can't find on the map, and the van's making weird noises. What if it breaks down?"

"It won't break down, Hallie. Trust me," said Adam.

Adam's words were cheering, but his voice

sounded uncertain. Hallie looked out the window and shivered.

Spring had come late this year after a long, harsh winter. It was now the end of April, and the cold, lashing rains had washed mud and old leaves down from the embankments onto the primitive, bumpy road they were traveling.

Hallie had never been in this part of the state before—the remote, mountainous area on its western border. There seemed to be little in the way of civilization out here. A few badly repaired roads, and a gas station many miles back. That must have been where they'd taken the wrong turn, gotten on the wrong road.

They'd been driving for six hours. Six long hours for a trip that was supposed to take only four. Something must have gone wrong. Seriously wrong. They were nowhere near their intended destination. And with the rains and the mist, twilight would come early.

We're lost, Hallie thought. *Not that Adam will ever admit it!* She heard the *ping* in the motor again. It seemed louder. *Maybe my imagination is working overtime.*

Almost as if she'd read Hallie's thoughts, the red-haired girl in the front seat turned and smiled reassuringly.

"Adam's van always makes weird noises, Hallie. It's a little eccentric, that's all."

A little eccentric? Hallie sat back in her seat and shook her head. Trust Becky to come up with something like that to describe her boyfriend's wheels.

Hallie could think of a few other words for that pile of junk. Words like *decrepit, dilapidated,* and *unsafe at any speed.*

So why on earth am I riding in it? she asked herself.

Because I didn't want to spend four hours on a school bus with the guy who just dumped me for the class flirt, that's why. My only regret is that I didn't drop him before he dropped me.

Hallie knew it would have been a long, tough bus ride if Becky hadn't invited her to drive to the Shakespeare Festival with her and Adam. The two girls had been best friends since fourth grade, and Becky could always be relied on to bail her out of trouble.

The Shakespeare Festival had seemed like a good idea when Mr. Costello, the drama coach, had announced it in assembly. Not only would the drama club be competing with students from all over the state, but they were excused from school on Friday in order to make the trip to

7

Harrington College. When Hallie had found out that they were doing a scene from *A Midsummer Night's Dream,* her favorite play, she'd thought the plan was perfect. And then Craig had decided to tell her he'd found true love with Kimberlee Beasley. So here she was, lost in the wilds, with Becky and Adam.

The road grew steeper. The old van was having a hard time of it now, bucking and wheezing as it mounted the hills. In the open area behind the seats the suitcases containing the teens' Elizabethan costumes for the play slid from side to side as the van maneuvered one sharp turn after another.

Hallie leaned back in her seat and watched Becky and Adam, envying them their easy closeness.

Adam and Becky. Becky and Adam. The two had been together for as long as Hallie could remember. Becky always said she was sure she and Adam had known each other in a previous incarnation.

Becky was like that. Dreamy. Romantic. Hallie often accused her of wanting to live in the past, and Becky agreed.

"I love anything old," she always said. "Sometimes I feel out of place in the twentieth century."

Hallie thought Becky even *looked* old-fashioned, with her long red hair and gorgeous complexion. She never seemed to get a big ugly zit or have a bad hair day like everybody else.

As the road twisted and looped higher and higher around the mountain, the rain turned to a thin drizzle, then stopped altogether, giving way to a mist that blanketed the road and hung from the branches of the low-lying shrubs like wispy, tattered cobwebs.

Adam slowed the van to a crawl and peered anxiously out from between the slow-moving windshield wipers. To make matters worse, the tree-covered area on their right had given way to a sheer drop. Hallie could see it through a hole in the mist.

"Uh, Adam," she said, feeling her stomach tie itself into a tight knot. "Do you think you could stay a little more to the left? There's quite a drop-off here."

"So I noticed," Adam responded. He slowed the van even further, keeping it as close to the middle of the road as he dared. Hallie could tell by his white-knuckled grip on the wheel that he was worried about meeting another car head-on. The *ping* in the engine had turned to an ominous clanking now.

"Look up there," Becky said, pointing to where the mist had cleared slightly. "The road seems to be widening out, and we've got ground and trees on our right again."

The knot in Hallie's stomach unraveled a little.

"There's even a spot where we can pull over and look at the map," she said. "Maybe one of you guys can figure out where we are. I sure can't."

Adam pulled the van over to the shoulder, turned off the motor, and took a deep breath.

Hallie passed the map over the seat to him and Becky. "See? There's the main road we were on. But then we turned off on a side road, and then onto this one, and I can't find either on the map. I don't have any idea where we are right now."

Adam and Becky bent over the map. Finally Adam said, "You're right, Hallie. I don't see this road, or the one before it, either."

"They must be too small to appear on a map," Becky said. There was a forlorn quaver in her voice when she added, "Let's face it. We're lost."

Lost. Hallie looked out the window. The swirling mist reminded her of the fog machine from last semester's production of *Brigadoon,* a play about a quaint little village with a curse on it.

Hallie's heart sank. It would be dark soon.

"Well, if worse comes to worst, we can always sleep in the van tonight," she said, trying to sound cheerful. "And we've got soda and sandwiches in the cooler, so we won't starve."

"Oh, no," Becky moaned. "The others must be at the college already. If we don't show up tonight, people will worry. Mr. Costello will probably call our parents, and my mom will have a fit!"

Adam reached over and took Becky's hand. "We're not lost, Becko. Every road has to go somewhere, right? So if we keep going, we're bound to find a town, or at least a gas station. Then we'll get directions and call the college to let them know we'll be late."

What a great guy, Hallie thought. *Why can't I find somebody like that? How come I'm always attracted to the sexy sleazoid types?*

They were preparing to pull out onto the road again when they heard the noise.

It sounded as bad as, if not worse than, Adam's van, and it chugged toward them out of the mist, like a time-warp phantom from a horror novel.

"Omigosh!" Adam cried. "A real Model T Ford!"

Hallie poked him. "Quick! Jump out and stop

it. Maybe the driver can help us."

Adam hastily threw open his door and jumped out, waving his arms. The Model T putted to a stop on the narrow gravel shoulder that bordered the opposite side of the road.

The man who stepped out of the car was middle-aged, of average height, and his hair was beginning to recede slightly. He seemed perfectly normal, but Hallie got an uneasy feeling just looking at him.

Adam had gone over to the old car and was talking earnestly to the driver.

"I'd better go help Adam," Becky said. "You know how he is about getting directions. He always forgets later if he's supposed to go left or right."

Hallie, watching from her window, saw the man do a double take when Becky walked up.

People always stared at Becky when they first met her, Hallie reflected. Not, of course, the way this guy was, with his blue eyes wide and his jaw practically hanging open. But there was definitely something about Becky that made people look twice. After all, not many girls had a head of hair that long and thick and red—not an orangy, carroty red, but the rich, warm red of a blazing fire, with all its shades and striations of color.

Hallie wondered again why the stranger bothered her so much, especially since he seemed willing to help them.

The man was now pointing in the direction they'd been headed and making motions that indicated to Hallie that the road would be leading downward. Hallie smiled. The sooner they got on flat ground, the better.

Adam kept nodding and smiling. Maybe they weren't too lost after all.

Hallie slid the van door open, crawled out, and walked over to the group. Her uneasiness about the stranger increased as she drew closer to him. For one thing, he had an odd, smoky odor about him. Even out here in the open and a couple of feet away from him, she could smell it. Only, she could tell this wasn't tobacco smoke. It wasn't so much unpleasant as it was puzzling. *Maybe it's some weird kind of incense,* Hallie thought.

"And then you'll come to a little town called Holyoake," the man was saying. "I don't know much about it. The people there keep pretty much to themselves, but it's bound to have a garage." He had an odd accent, Hallie noted—old-fashioned or something.

"Great!" Adam said. "Thanks. We were starting to get worried."

The man smiled slightly, and Hallie could see that his teeth were in bad shape. Then he turned his gaze full upon her, and again she had the peculiar sensation that there was something . . . *wrong* about him.

"Hi! I'm Hallie," she said, holding out her hand.

Wordlessly, still staring at her, he stretched out his hand in reply. Hallie saw the quick flash of a tattoo on his wrist, under his cuff, then it was gone. His handshake was cold and clammy, and Hallie had to resist the impulse to wipe her hand on her jeans.

"Well, thanks again," Adam said cheerfully. "We'll be okay now."

They walked back to the van and climbed in. Hallie continued to watch the stranger through the window. He didn't get into his car right away—he kept staring thoughtfully after them. At Becky in particular.

He was smiling.

THREE

"Boy, what a nice guy," Adam said, starting the van. It coughed weakly and died a couple of times before finally catching hold. Adam pumped the gas pedal, and with a protesting sputter, the van pulled out on the road.

"What did he say?" Hallie asked, feeling like a monster for disliking the roadside Good Samaritan.

"He says that if we follow this road down the mountain, we'll come to a little town where there's a gas station and a telephone. We can get directions to the college and call Mr. Costello to let him know where we are."

"Great!" Hallie said. "I was really getting

15

worried. The van sounds like it's starting to fall apart."

Adam nodded. "I didn't want to upset you girls, but something's going wrong under the hood. And I think it's getting worse. I'll have the mechanic at the gas station take a look at it."

"But what if it breaks down before we get to the gas station?" Becky asked.

"According to that guy, the road goes downhill after the next rise," Adam told her. "We can always coast into town if worse comes to worst."

The van barely made it up the next hill, but when it crested and started downhill, it shuddered into gear and began to roll smoothly.

As they swept around a wide bend in the road, the mist parted. Through a gap in the trees below, they glimpsed what looked like the thin white spire of a church.

"That's the best thing I've seen all day," Hallie said. "Civilization at last! Where there's a church, there's bound to be a town."

"I bet it's one of those little old towns with a village green and everything," Becky said dreamily. "I heard there are a lot of them in this part of the state, and some go way, way back. To the sixteen hundreds, even."

The road began to narrow again, and Adam

had to zigzag around the deep potholes that pocked the road.

"Whoever's responsible for road repair must have run out of money right about here," he said, barely missing one deep pit, and hitting another that flung them against their seat belts.

They all breathed a sigh of relief when they found themselves on flat ground once again, the mountain safely behind them.

They seemed to be in a valley now. Mountains rose up around them on all sides, and Hallie, craning her neck, looked back on the one they'd just come down. The road looked even more winding than she'd realized.

The mist had disappeared, but twilight was coming on quickly. The sides of the road were now heavily treed, cutting out what light remained. Adam turned on his headlights.

Hallie felt a deep, unreasonable sense of depression.

"Where's that little town we saw from up on the mountain?" Becky asked. "Didn't that man say it would be down here someplace?"

"It can't be much farther," Adam said. "We've twisted and turned so much coming down the mountain, I'm not sure *where* it is."

They continued on for several more miles,

seeing no signs of habitation, the road narrowing down into little more than a country lane. The van sputtered to a halt a couple of times, but Adam managed to get it going again by stopping on the shoulder of the road, raising the hood and banging on the motor.

Finally Adam stopped the car. He leaned forward and peered through the windshield.

The road had dead-ended into what looked like a primitive dirt road running in both directions. A quaintly lettered sign that said HOLYOAKE, POPULATION 400 was nailed to a tree, with an arrow pointing to the right.

"Holyoake?" Hallie asked. "Is that the name of the town with the gas station and the telephone?"

"Yes, I think that's what the man said," replied Becky.

"Let's not be picky," Adam said. "Any town will do."

The van made feeble, protesting noises as Adam eased it slowly onto the old dirt road.

"Hang in there, good buddy," he pleaded, patting the dashboard. "We're almost there."

Overhead, tree limbs met and entwined, creating an enclosed avenue and lending a feeling of unreality to the scene. After they had driven for a half mile or so, the overhanging trees disappeared, and the road ended abruptly in a clearing at the edge of a small town.

No, *town* wasn't the right name for the little cluster of houses up ahead, Hallie decided. That was too modern, too contemporary a word. Holyoake wasn't a town. It was a village. A quaint, picturesque little village.

Hallie felt the hairs on her arms rise for some strange reason.

Down the street a man was lighting the old-fashioned gas lamps that lined the village green.

A real village green. That ought to satisfy Becky, Hallie thought.

The houses that fronted the streets were all early colonial, all wooden, and uniformly painted white, with fanlight windows over the front doors.

"I was right!" Becky said excitedly. "These houses are definitely pre-Revolutionary!"

At that, the van expired. No amount of revving and cajoling could bring it back to life.

"That's it, I'm afraid," said Adam, taking the key from the ignition.

"Is it something serious?" Hallie asked.

"Probably not. Any good mechanic ought to be able to put it back in business again. It breaks down all the time, as you've probably noticed."

"Well, I'm glad it hung in there long enough to get us to civilization," Becky put in.

Adam got out of the car and looked around. "Let's hope this *is* civilization and that the weird-looking building up ahead is a gas station."

Hallie and Becky peered through the gloom in the direction he indicated. The building was flat-fronted, with a peaked roof and a large bay window. It appeared to be half country store, half gas station, with assorted wares displayed in the window and antiquated-looking gas pumps out front.

"I've only seen pumps like that in World War Two photos," Hallie said. "Do you think these are still working?"

"They'd better be," Adam said. "The van needs gas, along with everything else."

With Becky steering, Hallie and Adam pushed the van the few remaining yards down the street to the store.

No sooner had they pulled up beside the pumps than two middle-aged women in shapeless, unfashionable dresses emerged from the store.

They were obviously customers, Hallie noted, as they were carrying baskets of groceries on their arms. Baskets rather than paper bags. *How unusual,* Hallie thought. But she knew Becky would love the old-fashioned baskets.

Both women seemed surprised to see Hallie and Adam, nodding silently at them and regarding them intently from under lowered lashes. Hallie realized then that they probably didn't see many strangers out here in this remote place.

The women lingered in front of the store, adjusting their baskets, still watching Hallie and Adam from the corners of their eyes. Hallie almost laughed aloud at their furtive inspection.

Becky opened the door of the van and stepped out.

What happened next was puzzling.

The two women froze in midmotion and stared at Becky. At her pale, creamy skin. At her mane of blazing red hair.

Becky, who was gazing, entranced, out over the Green, watching the lamplighter as he moved from gaslight to gaslight, didn't notice the women's startled reaction.

But Hallie did. She reminded herself again that people usually took a second look at Becky, because she was so pretty and because her hair was such an unusual color. But not like this, not like Becky was some kind of freak. Those two women were acting downright weird. The way the man on the road had.

Hallie edged closer to Becky and glared at the women, who were now looking at each other, exchanging unreadable glances.

What's going on here? Hallie thought. *Am I overtired? I must be imagining things.*

The older of the two women turned to Adam, who had opened the hood of the van and was peering helplessly into its entrails. "Is there something wrong with your machine?" she asked.

Machine? What a peculiar thing to call Adam's van.

The woman spoke with the same sort of accent the man on the road had. That same odd, old-fashioned way of pronouncing vowels. Maybe it was it a regional thing.

"Is something wrong with your machine?" the woman repeated.

Adam pulled his head out from under the hood.

"You mean my van? There sure is," he said. "I hope you've got a good mechanic in this town."

"Oh, there's no one better than our Norman," the second woman said. "I'll go get him for you, if you wish."

This one spoke just like the other.

"Thank you," Adam told her. "I'd really appreciate it if Norman would take a look at this motor."

Becky reluctantly tore her gaze from the lamplighter and turned, smiling, to the women.

"Norman?" she asked, oblivious to the way they were looking at her. "Who's Norman?"

They exchanged another unreadable look before the younger one answered. She seemed surprised Becky even needed to ask the question. "Norman's very important to our village. He runs this store and gas station. And takes care of the village fire engine. He knows everything there is to know about machines and all those modern things."

Machines? Modern things? Hallie wondered if this poor woman had ever heard about the space program. Or television. Did they even have radios in this place? *And are we in the Twilight Zone or what?*

When the older woman went back into the store to get Norman, the other mumbled something about having an appointment with the minister and struck out across the Green in the direction of the church.

Hallie, watching her, was amazed at how quickly she was walking, considering the heavy basket she was carrying.

Ages seemed to pass, however, before Norman appeared. At one point Hallie thought she heard the faraway ring of a telephone and assumed he was tied up with a phone call.

"Don't forget," she reminded her friends, "we've got to call Mr. Costello as soon as we find out what's wrong with the van."

Norman finally emerged from the store, followed by the older woman, who nodded to them and promptly scooted off in the same direction her friend had taken.

Norman was a rumpled-looking man dressed in baggy overalls. Hallie wondered where he bought them. She'd never seen anything like them before—they looked like something out of the Great Depression. Norman was briskly businesslike, although his glance did rest a little longer than necessary on Becky, Hallie thought. Hallie was almost certain that his eyes narrowed when he looked at her friend, but at least he didn't gape at her the way the two women and the man on the road had.

Norman disappeared under the hood of the van and rummaged around for a long time, wiggling and testing things. Finally he resurfaced and closed the hood gently, wiping his hands on a towel that hung from his pocket.

"I'm afraid I've got bad news," he said. His accent was just like that of the two women.

"What do you mean, bad news?" Adam asked, his forehead puckering with worry.

"It's going to take me quite a while to get that machine running again," Norman said.

"How long?" Adam asked.

"I'm afraid I can't have it ready until tomorrow evening at the very earliest. Maybe not even then."

"Tomorrow evening?" Hallie repeated, aghast. "But tomorrow's Saturday, and the festival's over on Sunday. Our weekend will be ruined!"

"I can't believe it," Becky moaned. "What are we going to do now?"

"It's all my fault," Adam said. "I should have had that motor overhauled before we left home."

Hallie glanced at Norman and was startled by the expression on his face.

He didn't look at all sympathetic. In fact, he was watching them the way the man on the road had, with a half-smile on his lips, as if he were secretly pleased about something.

FOUR

The look vanished in the blink of an eye, and Hallie wondered if she'd imagined the sly smile and the secret, gloating expression.

She'd been having these paranoid feelings all afternoon. Ever since they'd gotten lost, in fact. Hallie frowned. She wasn't usually like this.

Adam was looking at her and Becky. "Well, you heard the man. Anybody have any ideas?"

"First of all," Becky said, "we've got to call Mr. Costello before he calls our folks. You know my mother. She'll go bananas if she thinks we're lost."

Norman looked uncomfortable when they asked him if they could borrow his phone.

"You can put the call on my repair bill," Adam said.

Norman shifted from foot to foot and scratched the back of his neck. "It's kind of embarrassing to admit this to city folk like you, but our phone system here in Holyoake is pretty old."

"It doesn't matter what your phones look like," Hallie said. "Just as long as we can call out to let our folks know we're okay."

"That's what I'm getting at," Norman replied. "You can't. The phones are down."

"What do you mean, down?" Becky asked.

"Well, ah—" Norman coughed and shuffled his feet again, looking at the ground. "We had a bad electrical storm yesterday. It . . . it knocked out the phone lines. It happens all the time—the phones break down whenever there's a storm. It's never a big problem to us, though. None of us need to call The Outside very often."

The Outside? Hallie thought that was a strange way of referring to people in the surrounding towns. If there *were* surrounding towns in this remote valley.

"If the phones aren't working, we're in real trouble," Adam said. "How long do you think it will take before they're fixed?"

"Oh, I don't know. A day or two, maybe,"

Norman said with a shrug, still looking down at his feet.

"A day or two?" Hallie's voice was shrill. "I can't believe this. There's got to be some way of contacting—" She almost said, "civilization," but managed to bite the word off just in time. Suddenly she remembered the faraway ringing she'd heard earlier.

"Are you sure the phones are down?" she asked. "I could have sworn I heard a phone ring in your store a little while ago—just before you came out."

"No, you couldn't possibly have heard anything like that," Norman hastily assured her, shaking his head vigorously. "Like I said, the lines are all down. Maybe you heard my timer. I was boiling up a dozen eggs on the hot plate. Some people like to buy them that way."

He looked up at her when he spoke, his eyes blue and guarded. With a shock Hallie realized he bore a distinct resemblance to the man they'd met on the mountain road. Same blue eyes. Same facial structure. Same build.

She thought about asking him if he had a cousin who owned a Model T Ford but decided against it. Surely the man back there would have told them if he had any relatives in Holyoake. In fact, he hadn't seemed to know much about the town at all.

Instead she said, "But we've got to get in touch with our folks as soon as possible. Maybe we could send a wire. Is there a telegraph office in town?"

"A what?" Norman said blankly.

And this is the man who knows all about machines and "modern things"? Hallie thought in disbelief.

Adam took over the questioning.

"Look, Norman," he said. "Here's the situation: we were supposed to be at Harrington College this afternoon. I guess you know where that is."

Norman looked doubtful. "I might have heard of it, maybe, but—"

"The problem is," Adam continued, "if we don't show up by tonight, people are going to worry about us. Is there any way we can get to a town where the phones are working?"

"A bus, maybe?" Becky asked.

Norman laughed aloud. "Oh, no, little lady. There aren't any buses hereabouts. Not many outsiders come to Holyoake, and we natives don't travel much. We like it right here."

Becky looked over at the Green and sighed

wistfully. "I can see why. Holyoake is so beautiful. It's like stepping back in time."

"Well, maybe someone could give me a lift to the nearest town," Adam suggested impatiently. "I could make a couple of phone calls and then come right back."

When Norman didn't reply, he added hastily, "I'd pay him, of course. Just like a taxi."

"That's not the problem," Norman said. "We'd do it for you free, if it was possible. It's just that few people around here even own a motor car."

"You're kidding!" Adam said. "How can anybody survive without a car?"

"We've got just about everything we need right here within walking distance," Norman explained. "Holyoake's kind of like a commune. We share everything, grow most of our own food, and make a lot of things by hand, so we don't have to go Outside much."

"A commune? You mean, one of those Hippie things they used to have back in the sixties?" Hallie asked.

"Well, in a way. Our people have lived here in Holyoake for a long, long time, so most of us are related by blood. That's why living like this works for us. We think of ourselves as one big family."

"Isn't that nice?" Becky put in. "This place is so darling."

"Look, surely *someone's* got a car I can use," Adam said.

"Like I told you, son, we don't have many cars here. Half of them don't work, anyway. And even if they did, everybody's pretty busy with the May Day festival—or Beltane, as we village folks call it—that's coming up on Sunday."

Norman fiddled absentmindedly with the towel that hung from his overalls before he continued. "It's not that we're inhospitable or unfriendly. It's just that Beltane is a pretty big social affair for us, and everyone's rushing around like crazy, trying to get things done."

"So that's it?" Hallie demanded incredulously. "It will be days before we can leave Holyoake, and there's no way of letting our folks know where we are in the meantime?"

Norman raised both hands, palms out, as if he were trying to keep Hallie from running off. "Now don't get all worked up, young lady. I think I have the answer to your problem. Could somebody make your call for you?"

"Sure," Becky said. "Just so people know we're okay."

"Well, Netty Talbot—she's our town librarian—

has been talking about having to go to the county seat to pick out some books for the school library. It wouldn't take much to persuade her to go tonight. She likes to get there the night before, anyway, so she can start in early the next morning. But she'll be staying in town all day, so I don't think one of you would want to go with her. I know she'd go tonight, if she thought she was helping you out."

"But this is pretty short notice, isn't it?" Becky asked. "I mean, with the festival and everything."

Norman shook his head and smiled. "If I know Miss Netty, she's done all her work for the festival in advance. And she's a spinster lady, so she doesn't have children or a man to worry about."

Spinster lady? Hallie thought. *There are still places in the world where a single woman is called a spinster lady?*

"Are you sure about this?" Adam asked eagerly.

"Yes, she's been talking about going for a couple of weeks now. This will give her a good excuse."

"What about a car?"

"She's got the little roadster her father left her. I just overhauled it, so she'll be wanting to try it out."

"I've got Mr. Costello's emergency number at the college," Becky said, reaching into the van and pulling out her carryall. "As long as he knows we're okay, he won't call our parents."

Becky wrote down the number for Miss Talbot, plus a short note, telling her what to say to Mr. Costello, and Norman said he would personally see that the librarian received it before she left. "Right after I get you kids safely settled for the night."

Becky and Hallie stared at each other. Of course. They'd have to find a place to spend the night. They'd been so busy worrying about everything else, they hadn't given a thought to where they'd sleep.

Norman caught the look that passed between them.

"That won't be a problem. Mrs. Grigsby over there—" he pointed to a house on the far side of the Green "—has some spare bedrooms. She's a nice widow lady, and I know she'd be glad to have you stay overnight. Especially if you're paying guests."

His voice dropped conspiratorially. "Mrs. Grigsby can use a little extra money. She hasn't got much more than that big old family house and a lot of pride. And she's got her teenage nephew, Simon, to support, too."

The expression on Norman's face when he

said Simon's name indicated he didn't think much of him.

"You wait here, though," he told them. "I'd better go ask her first. No sense all of us showing up on her doorstep."

"Isn't Norman sweet to do this for us?" Becky asked, watching him make his way across the Green toward a large house surrounded by a picket fence.

"People are like that in small, out-of-the-way places," Adam replied. "Helpful."

"But Holyoake is special," Becky said. "I can feel it. There's something about this place that really appeals to me."

Hallie didn't reply. It had grown dark. Twilight had turned to night, almost without her noticing it, while they'd been talking to Norman.

A chill wind had arisen, and it made a soft moaning sound as it blew across the open expanse of the Green. In the surrounding houses lights were winking on behind drawn curtains.

But before they did, in a couple of those houses, Hallie thought she'd seen the edges of the curtains move slightly. As though people were looking out.

Stealthily.

And at them.

FIVE

Norman was gone a long time.

"Maybe he's having a hard time talking her into it," Hallie suggested nervously. "Maybe Mrs. Grigsby's not as hard up for paying guests as he says."

Across the Green, lights flickered on in what was probably Mrs. Grigsby's living room, judging by the large front window. From where they were standing, the teens could see what looked like a number of people moving about in the room.

"Look," Becky said, pointing. "I think she's got company. Or maybe she has other overnight guests."

"I doubt it," Adam said. "Norman said they

don't get outsiders through here very often."

Suddenly someone walked over to the window and closed the curtains. It was an abrupt movement, almost as if whoever it was knew people were looking in and wanted to cut off the view.

When Norman finally returned, he was smiling. "Mrs. Grigsby's waiting for you. I'll help you carry your bags over."

"What about Miss Netty?" Hallie asked.

"What?" Norman said absentmindedly.

"When are you going to talk to her about driving over to the county seat and making that phone call for us?" Hallie reminded him. "She'll have to be starting soon, won't she?"

"Oh, that," Norman replied. "Right. I'll go over to Miss Netty's as soon as I get you three settled at Mrs. Grigsby's."

"I hope we won't be crowding Mrs. Grigsby," Becky said. "It looks like she has a bunch of other people there tonight."

Norman seemed puzzled. "What other people?"

"We saw them through the front window," replied Becky.

"There wasn't anyone there but me and Mrs. Grigsby. And Simon, her nephew. Maybe that's who you saw."

"It sure looked like more people than that," Becky said.

"That Simon," Norman said sourly, "has a way of filling up a room."

Mrs. Grigsby was plump and motherly with a sweet smile. And blue eyes just like Norman's. Hallie remembered what Norman had told them about everybody in Holyoake being related. That explained a lot. The two women they'd met in front of the store had eyes that same shape and color, too.

Mrs. Grigsby, like Norman and the women, had the same odd way of pronouncing some of her words. Hallie decided it must be a local thing, the result of being so isolated from the rest of the world.

"My goodness, children, you do have a lot of bags," Mrs. Grigsby said.

"We've got costumes in some of them," Becky explained. "We were supposed to be in a play this weekend, but I guess the show will have to go on without us."

Mrs. Grigsby shook her head sympathetically. "Yes, Norman told me. Well, if you had to break down anywhere, Holyoake's the best place for it. We'll take care of you."

"Be it ever so humble, there's no place like

Holyoake. Right, Aunt Phoebe?" said a mocking voice from the doorway.

Hallie turned to look. And then looked again.

This guy was gorgeous. Tall, dark, handsome.

He appeared to be her age, Hallie thought. Maybe a little older. But there was something dangerous about him.

Hallie was glad she was only going to be in Holyoake for the weekend.

Mrs. Grigsby's smile didn't waver as she viewed her nephew, but it seemed to go from sweet to sour, like curdled milk. "How nice of you to come and help with the baggage, dear. Children, I want you to meet my nephew, Simon."

Simon, lounging in the doorway, one broad shoulder resting on the doorjamb, favored them with a curt nod.

Hallie was aware he was looking them over. His glance lingered briefly and disapprovingly on Becky's red hair, slipped over Adam, and came to rest on Hallie.

She felt her cheeks go hot. She was acutely aware that her long black hair had escaped from its French braid and was hanging in messy wisps around her face. Not that it made the slightest difference what sort of impression she was making on him, of course.

Simon turned, and without a word, tucked a couple of bags under his arm and started up the stairs. There was something rude about the way he did it.

Mrs. Grigsby flashed an apologetic smile and fell in behind him, beckoning the teens with nervous little fluttering motions to pick up their bags and follow.

The staircase wound up to a landing and a long hall that ran the width of the house, with doors opening onto it. Simon turned left and led them down the hall, pushing open the door to a room on the far end.

"This one's yours," he said, turning to the girls.

"And that one across the hall is yours, dear," Mrs. Grigsby told Adam. "The bathroom is over there. I'm afraid you'll all have to share."

They sorted out their suitcases. Simon unceremoniously dumped Becky's and Hallie's on the floor beside the door. Then he disappeared. Hallie was surprised at how quickly and quietly he could move.

"Dinner in a half hour," Mrs. Grigsby told them. "Please don't be late."

The girls' room was large and overlooked the Green. Twin beds, both four-posters and undoubtedly antique, were covered with handmade quilts and heaped with ruffled pillows. A beautifully polished pine table holding a lamp and a shell-encrusted sewing basket served as a nightstand between the beds. The floorboards were dark and of random widths, undoubtedly the hand-hewn originals. The floor was dotted here and there with hand-braided scatter rugs in the same colors as the quilts.

"Look at this place," Becky said, her eyes shining. "Isn't it gorgeous?" She glanced over slyly at Hallie. "And speaking of gorgeous, what do you think of Mrs. Grigsby's nephew?"

Hallie carefully laid a couple of sweaters in a bureau drawer before replying. "He's pretty cute, I guess," she said casually.

Becky laughed. "I told you you'd perk up and forget about Craig once you met someone new and interesting."

"I am *not* perking up," Hallie retorted. "Not over Simon, anyway. He's new, all right. And I guess he might be interesting if you like macho, insensitive types. But he's probably one of the most unlikable guys I've ever met."

"My, my," Becky said, raising her eyebrows. "It sounds like you've been giving him a lot of thought."

*　　*　　*

Dinner was served on a long table in the dining room, and the room was lighted only by a cluster of the beeswax candles that Mrs. Grigsby said were made by hand in Holyoake.

The curtains to the dining room, Hallie was surprised to see, were open, and the candlelight was reflected in the wavy, dimpled glass of the windows. Hallie wondered how old that glass was. It had obviously been hand blown. Becky was right—everything about Holyoake made you feel as if you'd stepped back in time.

The night-darkened panes acted like a mirror, and Hallie could see Simon's profile from where she sat. Several times she glanced over and saw him watching her the same way.

Simon said very little at dinner. But his aunt was quite a chatterer. And very pleasant, Hallie thought, although sometimes she seemed almost a little *too* pleasant. And a little too flattering.

"What a lovely treat this is for us, having guests," she said, beaming down the length of the table. "And such beautiful young girls, too! Isn't that right, Simon?"

Simon muttered something affirmative and looked embarrassed. *The first human emotion he's shown since our arrival,* Hallie thought, chuckling inwardly at his discomfort.

Mrs. Grigsby burbled on. "No wonder you two girls are such good friends. You're both so pretty, each in your own way, and you complement each other with your coloring. You, Becky, with your blue eyes and your lovely hair, red as flame—"

Simon made an abrupt movement at that, which Mrs. Grigsby didn't seem to notice.

"And you, Hallie, with your black hair and gray eyes. What an unusual combination. So striking! You don't see that very often." Mrs. Grigsby paused and smiled. "At least not here in Holyoake. We all resemble our Saxon ancestors, I'm afraid. Blue eyes and pale-colored hair. We look as if we've all been cut from the same bolt of fabric."

Hallie looked over at Simon. Simon with his black hair and dark eyes. What bolt of fabric had *he* been cut from?

Mrs. Grigsby noticed Hallie's glance.

"Now and then one of our people marries someone with more exotic bloodlines, however," she said, "and we get someone like Simon. His mother was an Outsider and of Spanish descent."

Although she obviously had tried to sound warm and loving when she said that, it came off as just the opposite. As a condemnation of both Simon and his mother.

Hallie saw Simon's knuckles whiten as they gripped his fork.

He's always been a black sheep, Hallie thought. *No wonder he acts so hostile.*

After dinner, at Becky's urging, Mrs. Grigsby told them all about her home.

Simon had slipped away after supper, silent as a shadow. Adam looked as if he wished he had, too, judging from his yawns and looks of utter boredom. But Becky was hanging on Mrs. Grigsby's every word. It was obvious she'd fallen in love with the house and its furnishings.

"This house was built in seventeen hundred?" she asked. "Why, that's almost three hundred years ago! Is that when your ancestors came to Holyoake?"

"That's when all the local folks' ancestors came to Holyoake," Mrs. Grigsby replied. "They came here together."

Becky looked at her quizzically. "You mean, like in a group?"

"Yes. Our ancestors lived together on a small island off the northern coast of England. It was a very remote island. Very—" she paused for a moment "—very isolated. People clung to their . . . old ways."

"Old ways?" put in Adam, making a valiant effort to share Becky's interests.

"Yes," Mrs. Grigsby said. "Old beliefs. Old religious practices. That's why we were forced to leave England."

"Oh," Hallie said. "You mean your ancestors were like the Pilgrims. They came to America to escape religious persecution."

Mrs. Grigsby suddenly busied herself picking dead leaves from a floral arrangement. "Well . . . yes, dear. Something like that."

Hallie gave a startled little gasp when Simon materialized in the doorway.

"Yes, our ancestors were persecuted for their religious beliefs. Holyoake is a real pillar of righteousness when it comes to religious tolerance, isn't it, Aunt Phoebe?"

Hallie didn't miss the glance that passed between Mrs. Grigsby and her nephew. A flash of anger, anger tinged with a silent warning, on Mrs. Grigsby's part. A flat, defiant stare on Simon's, his lips curled in a faint sneer.

Once again Hallie was glad she had to hang around here only for the weekend. All this under-the-surface hostility was hard on the nerves!

She pretended to yawn broadly. "Would you mind if I called it a day? I got up awfully early this morning."

"Me, too," Adam chimed in, eager to escape. "I think I'll turn in, too."

Mrs. Grigsby nodded. "Of course. I should have realized you've had a long day. Besides, you'd better get some sleep while you can. The whole village will be up and rattling around under your window early tomorrow morning, getting ready for the Beltane festival. They'll be out on the Green, putting up the Maypole and stacking the kindling for the bonfire."

"Norman says you're celebrating May Day— Beltane—on Sunday," said Adam.

"Maybe we'll still be here for it. It sounds like fun," said Becky.

"Oh yeah, it's a real blast," Simon said with a black look.

Mrs. Grigsby's laughter was strained. "Don't let Simon fool you, children. He has more fun at our local celebrations than anyone."

There was an awkward pause. "You two go on upstairs without me," Becky told her friends. "I'd like to stay and talk to Mrs. Grigsby for a little bit." She turned to Mrs. Grigsby. "That is, if it's okay with you."

Mrs. Grigsby beamed. "Why, of course, dear. There's nothing I'd like better."

Becky still hadn't come upstairs by the time Hallie crawled into one of the twin four-posters. She fell asleep almost immediately, but awoke with a start when Becky came into the room, treading heavily and colliding with the bureau. After some fumbling around in the dark she slipped into the other bed.

"Beck?" Hallie called out. "What time is it?"

"I dunno," Becky said. Her voice sounded strange. Slurred.

Hallie raised her head from the pillow. "Becky? Are you all right?"

"Of course," Becky said, still in that odd voice. "I'm jus—just tired. Really tired. All of a sudden I got so sleepy."

"No wonder. You should have come to bed when I did," Hallie scolded. "What have you been doing all this time, anyway?"

Becky yawned, and when she spoke, her voice sounded as if it came from far away. "I was in the kitchen with Mrs. Grigsby . . . talking . . . herb tea . . . What a nice lady!"

She yawned again, then her heavy breathing told Hallie she'd fallen asleep.

Hallie fidgeted around, plumping up her pillow and rearranging her blanket in a vain attempt to get comfortable again. But it was no use—she was wide awake now.

She finally put her arms behind her head and stretched out her legs, trying to relax.

What a day! Lost in the mountains. And then stumbling upon this strange little village. And Simon.

Was something wrong with Becky? Hallie had seen her tired before, but not like this. Not drop-dead tired. Not slurring her words.

Hallie sighed and turned over on her side. Why did everything seem so grim in the middle of the night? The way Becky's voice had sounded, for example. It wouldn't take much to imagine Becky was under the influence of alcohol.

Or drugs.

SIX

Hallie finally gave up. It was no use. She couldn't fall asleep again. Becky's gentle snores from the next bed irritated her. How could Becky sleep so soundly when she, Hallie, couldn't? After all, it was Becky and her noisy clomping around and bumping into things that had woken Hallie.

She groped for her travel alarm clock. Once upon a time its dials had glowed in the dark, but those days were over. Try as she may, she couldn't make out the time.

Hallie threw back her covers and, still clutching the clock, tiptoed to the window. The wind that had arisen earlier was blowing scrappy little clouds across the face of the moon. She squinted at the clock and saw that its hands were joined.

Midnight. The witching hour.

Hallie sighed and knelt by the window, looking out.

The flickering lights of the gas lamps that ringed the Green illumined the gaunt, twisted branches of a huge old oak tree. She'd seen it when they'd first arrived in Holyoake, hunched in the twilight on the far side of the Green, like an evil presence.

She knew it was old. She'd noticed right away that it looked ancient, and that it was wired and propped up with forked limbs to keep it from falling down. Now, in the uncertain light of the gas lamps and a cloud-covered moon, there was something menacing about it.

She shivered. There was something eerie about this place, no matter how much Becky liked it.

A movement on the far side of the Green made her look beyond the oak tree, beyond the lights, toward the church. Yes, she could make it out now. There in the church. Something was going on.

Someone was entering the church, someone dressed in white. For a few brief moments the big double doors were opened wide, and Hallie could see people wearing what appeared to be long white robes, moving about in the tremulous light of—wait, those couldn't be torches, could they? Of course not. They were probably only candles.

Then the doors swung shut.

Hallie realized she was chewing on a thumbnail. It had all seemed so . . . unnatural. Maybe she should awaken Becky and—

No, forget that. She'd never be able to rouse Becky. She was out for the count, judging from the sounds she was making. Adam, maybe? No. What would Mrs. Grigsby say if she caught Hallie tapping furtively at his door at this time of night? Besides, what she was seeing was probably only a candlelight service of some sort. Those *had* to be candles, not torches.

She remembered what Mrs. Grigsby had said about her ancestors. How they'd come to Holyoake to escape religious persecution. Maybe her religion, whatever it was, involved a lot of ritual. That would explain white robes and candles and a mysterious midnight ceremony.

Every nerve in her body tingling, Hallie went back to her bed and crawled beneath the covers. She was even more wide awake now than before.

She'd never get to sleep at this rate.

I could sneak across the Green and peek in, she reasoned. *It isn't spying. Why should they mind, anyway?*

Quietly she got out of bed and pulled on a pair of dark sweatpants and a navy cotton sweater. Then she rammed her feet into her sneakers, tying them hurriedly, and left the room, pulling the door closed behind her.

She regretted not having a flashlight, but she could see the doors, pale as ghosts, on either side of the hall, and knew when she'd reached the landing.

The staircase, she remembered, was long and curving, but the stairs themselves were wide, and the treads shallow, so she knew that if she took her time and held fast to the railing, she'd be all right.

A board creaked as she rounded the bend in the stairway, and she paused, frozen like a rabbit caught in the glare of headlights, to see if she'd roused anyone.

Nothing. Good.

Still clutching the rail, she continued on down the stairs. She knew when she had reached the bottom, because a glimmer of light filtered through the fanlight window over the front door and lit up the last step.

There was a big brass bolt on the front door. Hallie had noticed it earlier, but fortunately it wasn't in place now—it would have been hard to slide the bolt without making a noise.

Hallie turned the handle slowly, easing the door open, and paused on the threshold, listening. Not a sound in the house. So far, so good.

Before she closed the door behind her, she checked to make sure she wouldn't lock herself out. She'd hate to spend the night in Mrs. Grigsby's azalea bushes.

She stood for a moment, clinging to the railing of the front stairs, and looked across the Green at the church.

The candlelight ceremony was still going strong. The faint sound of singing floated across the Green. It was a tuneless monotone sound, more like chanting than singing. A strong male voice would call out something, and the congregation would answer in an eerie, one-note chant.

Hallie took a deep breath and started across the Green. Why did she feel so nervous about this? The members of the congregation would probably be happy to see her there.

Nevertheless she found herself hugging the

shadows of the trees that bordered the Green so no one could see her approaching.

The voices grew louder as she neared the church. The doors were closed, but flickering shafts of light leaked out across the sill.

What was it they were chanting in there? Maybe she should listen before she opened the double doors. She might be arriving at the wrong moment in the ceremony.

She paused beside the bush that grew by the entry stairs and cocked her head, listening.

What was that word they repeated over and over again, like a litany? Goddess? Surely she was misunderstanding them. Maybe they were only saying "goodness" in that odd accent they all seemed to have.

And yet, for some reason, Hallie still hesitated to enter the church. Instead she walked softly around to the side of the building. *There must be windows here.* Maybe if she stood on tiptoe, she could see in.

The windows, however, were shuttered, and only a little light showed around their edges. It was dark here—and spooky, with those voices droning on and on in that creepy monotone.

Suddenly a figure loomed up out of the surrounding darkness, grabbed her arm roughly, and clamped a hand over her mouth.

"What are you up to, you sneak?" an angry voice hissed in her ear.

Simon!

Hallie's heart had nearly stopped when he'd reared up like an avenging demon. But now it was beating furiously, powered by the adrenaline of anger. She tried to pull free of his grasp, but he was too strong for her.

"If I take my hand away from your mouth, do you promise not to yell?" he said in a low voice.

She nodded. When he removed his hand, she whispered hotly, "What are you doing, sneaking up on me like this? Let go of my arm!"

"What are *you* doing," he retorted, not releasing her, "prowling around, dressed like a cat burglar?"

"Let go of my arm," Hallie repeated. "Let go or I'll scream my lungs out!"

He hastily let go. "Okay. Now answer my question."

"I . . . I saw the church from my window. And I saw the people in the white robes," she said, rubbing her arm. "So I thought I'd come over and—"

"And spy on them, I suppose," Simon said in a low, harsh voice.

He gripped her arm again, tighter this time, and pulled her toward him. The physical violence of it frightened her. "If you know what's good for you, you'll go back to bed and mind your own business. Nobody asked you to come here to Holyoake and snoop around."

Then he pushed her from him. She staggered for a second and almost fell, but he didn't put out an arm to save her.

There were so many things she wanted to say to him. Things that would put him in his place and make him ashamed of the way he was treating her.

The only trouble was, she couldn't think of them at the moment.

Without a word she turned and made her way across the Green, into the house, and up the stairs as quickly and silently as she could in the dark, tears of humiliation and anger streaming unchecked down her cheeks.

SEVEN

When Hallie entered the dining room for breakfast the next morning, she was relieved to see that Simon wasn't there. Mrs. Grigsby, chirpy and twinkly as ever, waved her to the table where Adam was happily demolishing a plate of country sausage and scrambled eggs.

"What's Becky doing?" he asked, looking up. "Making herself beautiful?"

"She was still sleeping when I left our room," Hallie said, taking a seat. "I tried to wake her up, but she didn't even budge."

Mrs. Grigsby smiled. "Let the dear child sleep. I'll fix her something when she comes down."

Hallie noticed dirty dishes and a crumpled

napkin at the end of the table. Simon's place. He must have eaten and run. Hallie breathed a sigh of relief.

Mrs. Grigsby noticed her glance. "Simon's gone out to help with the Beltane preparations. The old oak tree needs more propping up. It's starting to lean again."

"I noticed the tree last night before it got dark," Hallie told Mrs. Grigsby. "It looks terribly old."

"It is," said Mrs. Grigsby. "That's the oak the town is named for."

"The town was named for that tree?" asked Adam. "Why?"

"Well, when our ancestors came to America, their—" she paused for a brief second "—their *pastor* came with them, and he brought a seedling oak from the grounds of the old village's place of worship. He planted it right out there, on what would become the Green. As you can see, it's still standing, even after nearly three centuries. So eventually the village came to be called Holyoake, because of the tree."

"But why holy?" Adam asked.

"Back in pagan times the oak tree was considered sacred," explained Mrs. Grigsby. "Our ancestors were descended from one of the old pagan tribes. Old habits and traditions die hard around here. Or maybe the oak was called holy simply because it grew on the grounds of our ancestors' old place of worship. Who knows?"

Mrs. Grigsby's blue eyes had become shuttered, unreadable, when she'd spoken of the oak. Hallie wondered why.

Then, quickly changing the subject, Mrs. Grigsby said, "You two must meet Reverend Thoreson. He's our . . . vicar. We've always had a Reverend Thoreson here in Holyoake. It's one of those callings that have been passed down from father to son."

Becky finally appeared, just as Adam and Hallie were preparing to leave the dining room. Hallie noticed that Becky looked a little pale and that the skin around her eyes seemed a bit puffy.

If Adam noticed a change in Becky's appearance, he didn't comment on it. "I'm going to go see Norman about the van," he said, pushing back his chair. "Maybe it's not as bad as he thought. Maybe we can still make it to the Shakespeare Festival. Even if it's only for the last day."

Keeping a wary eye out for Simon, Hallie ran back upstairs while Becky ate her breakfast. He was nowhere in sight. Maybe he was as embarrassed about what happened last night as she was. *He should be,* she thought grimly.

When she came down the stairs for the second time that morning, Hallie found Becky in the kitchen, perched on a stool and listening, entranced, to Mrs. Grigsby talk about her herb garden.

"Oh, Hallie," she cried when she spotted her friend. "Mrs. Grigsby is an herbalist. She's been telling me about some of the things she does with herbs. She's kind of like the local medicine woman. It's so fascinating!"

Mrs. Grigsby beamed modestly. "I do my best. It's a wonder what can be done with herbs. My old granny was a healer, so she taught me everything she knew."

"This house even has an herb room," Becky told Hallie. "It's the little room off the back hall. Mrs. Grigsby says I can visit it later this morning, when she's working out there."

Hallie waited for Mrs. Grigsby to extend the invitation to her, too, but Mrs. Grigsby suddenly got very busy scrubbing out her already spotless sink. Hallie was more amused than insulted. She wasn't all that interested in herbs anyway. Besides, she was glad that Becky, at least, would be enjoying their stay here in Holyoake.

"Then how about taking a walking tour of the village with me in the meantime?" she asked Becky. "Everyone's out on the Green, getting ready for the festival. It should be interesting."

"Oh yes, do," said Mrs. Grigsby, pausing in her scrubbing. "You can meet some of the villagers. I'm sure Reverend Thoreson will be there supervising the arrangements. What a *lovely* man! He'll be directing the pageant tomorrow."

"Pageant?" asked Hallie.

"It's quite a do, really," Mrs. Grigsby explained. "There will be games and food and a great bonfire on the Green. Everyone comes in medieval costumes, the way they have for centuries here in Holyoake."

As Becky and Hallie walked across the Green, the groups of people they passed fell silent and stared at them. Particularly at Becky. It wasn't the staring that bothered Hallie the most. It was the strange pleased, secretly excited expressions on the villagers' faces that unnerved her. And the way their eyes lingered on Becky's thick, fire-colored hair. For the umpteenth time since leaving home the day before, she wondered if no one had ever seen a redhead in this part of the state. But no—there was one, right over there, although *her* hair was a pale, carroty color.

"I feel like a Thanksgiving turkey just before they bring out the cranberry sauce," she whispered to Becky.

Becky laughed. "They're just curious, Hallie. Mrs. Grigsby says they don't see many outsiders here in Holyoake."

"I don't get it," Hallie muttered hotly. "Why should they be so darn curious? They don't *have* to shut themselves away from civilization, do they? And what's more—"

"Sshhh!" Becky cautioned, elbowing Hallie to silence.

A sandy-haired man was making his way rapidly toward them over the smoothly clipped surface of the Green. Although he was tall and broad-shouldered, his eyes and the bone structure of his face resembled that of Norman and Mrs. Grigsby.

"Good morning, ladies," he said.

His voice, as Hallie had expected, was typically Holyoake.

"My name is Joshua Sidlaw," he explained. "I'm one of the twelve village elders. Reverend

Thoreson has asked me to give you a little tour of the village. We've all heard of your coming and hope you are enjoying your stay here in Holyoake."

"How thoughtful! Isn't that thoughtful, Hallie?" Becky asked.

"Yes, it is," Hallie said. "But you really don't have to do that, Elder Sidlaw."

"Nonsense, I want to. Now, where would you like to go first?"

"We've been watching the people get ready for the festival. What do they have to do before tomorrow?" Becky asked.

"Most of the preparations have already been completed," answered the elder, "but there are still many last-minute things. See the people over there at the oak?"

"Yes," Hallie answered. "Mrs. Grigsby told us about that tree and how old it is."

"Then you'll understand why they are busy at work propping it up. We're trying to keep it standing for as long as we can."

Hallie looked for Simon among the group. He wasn't there. Simon certainly knew how to maintain a low profile.

Maybe he saw me coming and ran—the rat!

Elder Sidlaw pointed to some women who

were approaching the oak, carrying flower garlands. "When the men have made the oak secure, these ladies will decorate it with wreaths of spring flowers. That's an old tradition here in Holyoake."

"Mrs. Grigsby said back in the old days people used to think oak trees were holy," Becky put in.

Elder Sidlaw looked at Becky for a moment before answering. "Yes, that's true. Our people used to worship oak trees . . . among other things."

A few yards beyond the tree, a Maypole was being erected. A deep hole had been dug, and several men were sinking the pole into it. Long, colorful ribbons fluttered down its top.

"That's another Beltane custom—the Maypole. The Maypole dance is supposed to ensure fertility," he said.

"What's going on over there?" Becky asked, pointing to the center of the Green, where a large group of people were laying wood—and something else—in preparation for the huge bonfire Mrs. Grigsby had told them about.

The something else, Elder Sidlaw explained, were bones. Cattle bones.

"Eeeuw!" Becky said. "How gross!"

"Not really," the elder explained, looking a little injured at Becky's reaction. "This is the center, the very heart, of the old Beltane festival. Again, it dates back to our pagan ancestors, who burned the bones of animals each year on the feast of Beltane."

"Why?" Becky asked. "And where do you get all those bones?"

"Whenever we butcher an animal—and we raise all our own meat here, on the farms just outside the village—we save its bones."

Becky still looked puzzled, so he hastened to explain.

"The word *bonfire* comes from the word *bonefire.* In the old days the festival of Beltane was supposed to herald in summer and the growing season. So it was a sacred ceremony. The bones of animal—and human—sacrifices were burned, and the ashes were then spread over the fields to ensure plentiful and healthy crops."

"*Human* sacrifices?" Hallie gasped. "You mean, they actually burned *people?*"

Elder Sidlaw nodded.

"And you're still celebrating a feast where things like that were done?"

"Why not?" Elder Sidlaw replied calmly. "It's an ancestral tradition. Afterward the entire village turns out to spread the ashes of the Beltane fire over the fields of Holyoake's communal farms. That's a tradition, too."

Hallie and Becky watched as a low platform with a stake in its center was erected in the middle of what would become the Beltane bonfire.

"I can't believe what I'm seeing," Hallie said. "This looks like they're getting ready for the real thing. Aren't you all carrying tradition just a bit too far?"

"It's totally harmless," the elder assured her. "In primitive times a maiden would have been sacrificed to the people's patron Goddess on Beltane. Now, of course, a straw dummy represents the maiden. It's just one of those peculiar customs, like the straw effigies they burn in England on Guy Fawkes day."

Becky was staring at the scaffolding, her eyes wide.

"Burned at the stake! What an awful way to die! I can't think of anything worse," she said in a horrified voice. "Even if I believed in some Goddess and all that baloney, I still wouldn't want to die like that."

Someone beckoned to Elder Sidlaw from across the Green.

"Oh dear," he said. "I believe I'm needed. I'll

be back just as soon as I can." He hurried off.

Becky looked at her watch. "Mrs. Grigsby said to come to her herb room so she can show me what she's doing before she has to stop and fix lunch. Do you want to come, too, Hallie?"

"No, thanks," Hallie said, remembering how Mrs. Grigsby had pointedly refused to issue her an invitation. "I'm going to walk around here for a while. Maybe I'll go visit that lovely old church on the edge of the Green."

"Don't be too long," Becky said. "I think I've seen enough. I love the village, and the people are all darling and friendly, but they *do* have some pretty gruesome traditions, don't they?"

When Becky left, Hallie started across the Green to the church. On the way she noticed a couple of small children sitting on the grass, playing listlessly with some wooden, hand-carved, farm animals. With a start, she realized these were the first children she'd seen in Holyoake so far.

How strange, she thought. *You'd think all the kids in town would be out here watching the preparations for the festival.*

She wondered if there was a bad case of flu going on in town, and if the other children were all sick in bed. These kids didn't look very healthy. They were pale and thin and listless. Frowning, Hallie turned back toward the church.

And then she saw him.

Standing half-hidden in the shadows of the church was the man they'd met on the road. Hallie was sure of it. The one who'd given them directions to Holyoake.

What was he doing here? He'd said he didn't know much about Holyoake, and yet here he was. Maybe he even lived here—he looked just like all the other people in the village.

He glanced in Hallie's direction, and she raised an arm to wave to him. She wasn't prepared for what happened next.

Even from this distance she could see the expression that came over his face when he recognized her.

He looked horrified.

Then he turned and ran.

EIGHT

Hallie watched, dumbfounded, as the man disappeared from view, like a cockroach scuttling down a drain.

"What's *that* all about?" she asked herself aloud. "What's with these people, anyway?"

As she drew closer to the old church, she noted that it looked exactly like every little white church in every small town in America. Picturesque. All-American. Reassuring.

But inside it was something else.

Hallie pushed open the heavy, creaking door and was immediately struck by a sudden chill and the sensation of . . . what? Of being lost? Trapped?

There was an unpleasant smell. Like bitter herbs mixed with burnt grass or straw. She wondered if it was some strange type of incense.

She remembered what Elder Sidlaw had told her about burning straw effigies for the festival. Surely they weren't doing it in here!

Whatever this building looked like on the outside, it was clear to Hallie that inside it definitely was *not* a church. At least not like any she'd ever seen.

Her eyes quickly adjusted to the gloom, and she took a few hesitant steps down what in another place might be called an aisle, passing row after row of thick, hand-hewn oaken benches. The benches were backless. Uncomfortable looking. The wilted remains of what looked like a garland of leaves lay on the floor beside one of them. It was crushed, as if it had been carelessly trod upon by a heavy foot.

She picked it up and laid it on the bench. Then, looking around her, Hallie saw something that made her heart beat faster.

All along the walls, on both sides of the room and at regular intervals, were heavy iron sconces holding unlit torches. The walls around them were black with their soot, indicating they were used regularly. So she'd been right after all.

Those *hadn't* been candles last night.

She knew she should leave this oddly frightening place immediately, but she couldn't. Something held her here. She stood in the aisle and looked straight before her at the front of the room.

A long black table made of dull, crudely hewn stone stretched across the width of the building. Along one side, facing her, were twelve high-backed, thronelike chairs. A thirteenth chair, more regal and thronelike than the others, sat at the end of the table, close to what appeared to be a primitive pulpit.

The gloom and lack of air—that smell of burnt torches and incense—and the feeling of oppression that had come over Hallie when she'd first entered the building made her feel a little dizzy, and she reached out for something to steady herself.

She found herself clutching what appeared to be a white marble baptismal font. Only, it was huge, too large, certainly, to be a font.

A deadly chill struck her as she looked into its depths. The bowl of the font was stained a deep rust color. Rust, the color of . . . blood?

"What are you doing in here?" boomed a voice, and Hallie almost leapt out of her skin.

"This Place of Worship," said the voice, "is not open to strangers!"

A thin, white-haired man stepped out from behind the carved wooden screen that backed the black table. At first glance Hallie thought he was old, because of the color of his hair. But as he drew closer, she saw his face. Although pinched and pale, it was that of a middle-aged man. He was dressed all in black, accenting his pallor, and his eyes were a peculiar silvery gray.

Hallie stared at him, speechless, and his grim expression relaxed a little.

"Forgive me. I didn't mean to frighten you," he said, inclining his head slightly. "I am Arthur Thoreson, the vicar of Holyoake."

When Hallie still didn't reply, he said, "I was startled to see someone—a stranger—in here. The church is usually kept locked. One of the elders must have been careless."

"I . . . I'm sorry," said Hallie. "I didn't realize . . ."

"This is an old, strict sect," the vicar said. "One must be a member to have access to the church. I'm sorry to have leapt out at you like that. I thought I was alone—I'm afraid you surprised me as much as I surprised you."

Then, taking Hallie's elbow, he escorted her back down the aisle and out into the sunlight.

Hallie was amazed at the swiftness with which he'd gone from stern to charming. And at the smooth, polite, yet firm way he managed to herd her out of the church.

Not that she minded. If those were the rules, she would be only too glad to play by them. She was happy to get out of that dank, dismal place and had no desire to set foot there ever again.

I've got too wild an imagination to go visiting places like that, she scolded herself. *As for that font, the rust in the local water must have stained it like that. It certainly couldn't have been caused by . . . anything else.*

"So good-bye for now, my dear," the vicar said with a small bow when they parted. "I understand you will be spending the weekend with us, so I'm sure we will meet again. I do hope you enjoy the festival. Beltane has been celebrated by our people for hundreds of years, so you will have the opportunity to participate in something rarely seen by Outsiders."

What a strange-looking man Reverend Thoreson was, Hallie thought as he left her. When he'd taken her arm to walk her out of the church, she'd noticed a tattoo on his wrist. She'd only seen it for a moment, but it appeared to be an image of flames. She'd never seen a clergyman with a tattoo before. And those eyes! That odd shade of pale silvery gray. They'd be unusual anywhere, but especially here in Holyoake where everyone had the identically shaped round blue eyes.

Warlock's eyes . . . The words leapt into her mind, as if someone had whispered them.

Instead of returning to Mrs. Grigsby's, Hallie made her way along the uneven brick sidewalk that led from the church to Norman's store and garage to see how the repair of the van was coming.

She entered the store, letting the screen door slam closed behind her. Inside it was dark, cool, and deserted, but there was an open door at its far end, and she could hear the distant sound of voices.

She walked the shadowy length of the building, past the refrigerated food area, with its displays of slab bacon, ground meat, and cheeses. Past the hardware section and its gardening supplies and out the rear door, still following the voices, to a weather-beaten old shed that was obviously Norman's garage.

The hood of the van was open, and Norman

and Adam were peering into its yawning cavity. Various bits and pieces of the engine were arranged neatly on a grimy cloth spread on the ground.

Adam looked up and beckoned Hallie over.

"Norm's replacing one of the hoses right now. The old one had holes in it," he said, gesturing to a rubber tube.

Hallie looked where he pointed. The old one had holes in it, all right, holes she didn't remember seeing the last time she'd looked into the innards of the van.

"It's even worse than we thought, Hallie," Adam told her gloomily. "The fuel pump's shot, too, among other things. Norman has to order a new one."

"I thought you said the fuel pump was new when you bought the van," Hallie said.

"That's what the guy who sold it to me said. He pulled a real fast one, that's for sure."

"How long will it take to get a new one?"

"At least a couple of days," Adam replied. "There's no chance we can make the Shakespeare Festival now. We'll be stuck here until Tuesday maybe."

"I'm glad Miss Netty contacted Mr. Costello for us. But we're going to have to get word to our folks, too, at this rate. Even if Mr. Costello tells them we're all right, they'll expect us to call."

"The phones are still down, Norman says," Adam told her.

Norman came out from under the hood. "That's right," he said, wiping his hands on a rag.

"I don't understand why it's taking so long to repair them," Hallie said.

Norman shrugged. "They're old. That's just how they are."

Before Hallie left, Adam said he had something to show her. "It's here, next door," he said. "You've got to see it to believe it!"

All that enthusiasm meant only one thing, Hallie thought. Some kind of four-wheeled vehicle.

Behind the garage was another shed. Its roofline was lower than that of the garage, so Hallie hadn't noticed it when she'd come out of the store. Adam took her around to its far side and threw open the double doors.

"Here it is, Norman's pride and joy," he said, leading her inside.

Hallie saw a large red truck of some sort, with a blunt-nosed cab and a big round tank on the back. It was old, by the looks of it, but well-kept and newly painted.

"What is it?" she asked. "An old fuel truck?"

"No. It's a water tanker. And in mint condition. I can't believe there are still any of these around, much less in use."

"A water tanker?"

"You know. An old-time fire engine that carries its own water."

He seized her hand and led her around to the back. "See, it's got a pump and hoses on the back. Isn't it neat, Hallie? You only see stuff like this in old pictures. And you're not going to believe it, but this—*this!*—is Holyoake's fire department, and Norm's the fire chief."

"You mean this thing really puts out fires?"

"Norm says it does. He's real proud of it. I'm surprised he doesn't put it on display at the festival."

"I wonder why Norman didn't volunteer to drive us to the next town in this," Hallie said thoughtfully. "He knew how badly we needed to get to a phone."

"Listen, Hallie, I bet Norm doesn't even drive this thing to a fire. It's kind of like his baby, you know? Besides, he sent Miss Netty, didn't he?"

As Hallie neared Mrs. Grigsby's house, she thought she heard a phone ringing. Delighted that the phones were finally working, she ran up the front steps and through the door.

Simon was standing by the telephone table in the hall, the phone to his ear. "Okay," he was saying in a low voice. "I'll be there."

He replaced the receiver and spun around guiltily when Hallie said, "Thank heaven the phones are working again. Do you think your aunt would mind if I placed a long-distance call?"

"Not at all," Simon said, "but you wouldn't get anyone. The ring you heard was from the repairman. That's who I was talking to. The lines are still down."

"I don't believe you," Hallie said coldly.

She pushed him aside and put the receiver to her ear. For one brief second she heard a dial tone. Then it went dead.

Simon went over to the window and drew aside the curtain. "See? Would I lie to you, Hallie?"

Hallie reluctantly joined him at the window. She rubbed her arm, remembering last night and not wanting to get that close to Simon again. The guy was a maniac.

"Up there," he said.

Hallie looked. A man was up on the telephone

pole. A man wearing a leather belt with tools hanging from it.

But is he fixing the line or disconnecting it? Hallie wondered darkly.

NINE

The twelve elders are gathered in a private, secluded room in the vicarage. Heavy, woven drapes are drawn to keep out the morning sun, and the room is lit only by the dim wattage of an antiquated hanging lamp.

The men's shadows loom large against the walls, and the sounds of the people out on the Green echo only faintly in this darkened room.

Someone else is present. Simon.

"You were supposed to keep that gray-eyed one occupied this morning," the vicar says accusingly to Elder Sidlaw. "Instead I caught her prowling around in the Place of Worship. Is this how you perform your appointed duties?"

"I was called aside briefly, and when I returned, she was gone," says Elder Sidlaw. "I thought she'd gone back to Sister Grigsby's place."

"No, she headed directly to the Place of Worship," says the vicar. "But first, she accidentally ran into that fool, Brother William. He'd been told specifically to remain out of sight. And then he made things worse by running from her. He came straight to me with the news, and I sent him upstairs for now, where he can't be seen."

"Brother William, the one who lured her here?" asks one of the elders. "Did the girl suspect anything?"

"I don't know," replies the vicar. "But it didn't stop her from entering our holy place. Fortunately I was there and saw her snooping around the sacrificial font. I got her out of there as quickly as I could. We can't run the risk of her discovering our plans at this point."

"So what if she does?" asks Elder Sidlaw, still smarting from the vicar's earlier rebuke. "Those three can't leave town without our catching them, and the phone lines have been disconnected, haven't they?"

"Yes, a few minutes ago," Simon says.

The older men regard him disapprovingly. The boy should know his place and speak only when spoken to.

"But those lines should have been disconnected last night," Simon continues, disregarding the elders' reproving looks. "Hallie's a smart girl. I'm surprised she didn't try to use the phone this morning."

He faces the vicar and says accusingly, "And she walked into the house when you were talking to me just now. We all agreed no one was to phone anyone else so the lines would appear to be dead. That call was bad timing on your part. You might have known she'd be coming through the door right about then."

The elders shudder with horror at the boy's rudeness. How will their vicar deal with this?

The vicar turns his compelling, silvery-gray gaze on Simon. "Don't you ever—ever—criticize anything I do or any decision I make. Had it not been for me, you would have been dead these many years. In return you owe me unquestioning loyalty and obedience. Is that clear?"

Simon bows his head obediently. "Yes, sir," he replies. "I'm sorry."

The elders nod at one another. The proper order of things has been restored.

"You're sure this will never happen again?" the vicar demands, reinforcing his authority.

"Yes, sir, I am," says Simon.

"You have a proud, willful spirit, Simon. We must all help you conquer it."

"It won't happen again," Simon tells him. "And I'll be more careful of what I say in the future."

"Good," says the vicar. "Now then, what about the other one? Our Fire Maiden."

"Aunt Phoebe's taking care of her," replies Simon. "She's introducing Becky to her most potent herb tea this morning. The girl will be putty in Aunt Phoebe's hands from here on out."

"Becky. Rebecca," the vicar says dreamily. "What a lovely name! Did you know that its old meaning is a noose, or a joining cord of some kind? How very fitting that this Rebecca, who has been so mercifully sent to us, will serve to join us once again to our beloved Mother Goddess."

"And what will we do, then, with the other two—the boy Adam and that little snoop, Hallie?" asks Elder Sidlaw.

Reverend Thoreson shakes his head regretfully. "What a pity they are so eager to leave us! They would have been real assets to our community. Fresh blood. That Hallie would have been a real match for you, Simon," he adds, laughing.

Simon blushes. Even in the dim light of the hanging lamp, the others can see the color that rushes to his face, and they laugh, too.

"But," the vicar continues, "that is impossible. Norman's clever story about contacting their families will hold them for only a short time. We can't risk keeping them around after the festival. The first time an Outsider passes through the village, they will be all over him, spilling our secrets."

"You mean . . . ?" Simon asks.

"Yes," replies the vicar. "And you know what happens to those who betray Holyoake, don't you, Simon? They are disposed of. Permanently."

He tips his head and regards Simon silently for a moment. "And this time I think it's appropriate that you do the disposing."

TEN

Becky wasn't around when Hallie went up to their room. *She's probably still with Mrs. Grigsby in her herb room,* Hallie figured. What was so interesting about herbs, anyway? And how could Becky drink those foul-smelling concoctions Mrs. Grigsby brewed up?

Mrs. Grigsby had said that lunch wouldn't be served until one o'clock, so Hallie went down to the living room, hoping to find Becky.

The room was deserted, but sunshine streamed through the windows, and the pleasant scent of last night's pinewood fire still lingered.

Hallie picked a book at random off one of the bookshelves and settled herself on the sofa. The book seemed quite old, but that didn't surprise her. So was everything else in Holyoake. It was the title, *Herbs for Amulets and Enchantments,* embossed in tarnished gold letters on a cracked leather cover, that made her uneasy.

Amulets? Enchantments?

She opened the book carefully, not wanting to loosen its already-damaged spine, and turned the pages.

What *was* this stuff? Where did Mrs. Grigsby get something like this? There was a long chapter on "Wortcunning," the Saxon name—it said—for knowledge of herbs and plants. It came complete with an incantation for fertility.

Hallie read on. There were instructions on how to tie bunches of certain herbs with red wool, because red is the color of fire and blood and—

Suddenly the book was snatched from her hands.

She hadn't heard Simon come into the room. Without a word, he walked across the room and returned the book to its spot on the shelf.

"How dare you!" she snapped, nearly overcome with rage. "What an incredibly rude thing to do. Don't they teach you manners in Holyoake?"

"Obviously more than they teach you where you come from," he replied.

"What's that supposed to mean?"

"It's supposed to mean that in a town like Holyoake, we value our privacy. We don't like people poking around in our living rooms. That book was Aunt Phoebe's private possession, and she wouldn't like an Outsider reading it and thinking she was some kind of a nut. And while we're on the subject, we don't like Outsiders coming into our church, either, like it was a public bus station or something."

"Outsiders! I'm getting sick of that word. What's the matter with you people anyway? Do you think you're all alone on this planet, and the rest of us are aliens from outer space?"

She was gratified to see him blush. He certainly *was* good looking. What a shame he was such a pain in the neck!

"And besides," she continued, "who told you I went into your church, anyway?"

"This is a small town, in case you haven't noticed," he said with a sneer. "Everybody knows everything that happens around here."

He leaned closer, and she noticed how very dark and intense his eyes were. "And maybe it's because this town was built around the church, but we take our . . . religion . . . pretty seriously. It's private. Sacred. And just for us. Know what I mean?"

Hallie nodded cautiously, her eyes wide. *This guy scares me,* she thought. *Is he crazy or what?*

"So how much longer are you going to be in town?" Simon asked abruptly.

Hallie cleared her throat. Her voice wobbled a little when she answered, but her words were defiant. "You ought to know, since you seem to know everything else that goes on around here. But, just in case you missed something, we can't leave until Norman fixes the van. According to him it will take a couple of days."

Then she glared at him and added, "And believe me, that van can't be ready a minute too soon."

"If you're that anxious to leave, why don't you go on foot?" Simon suggested. "There's a little road that goes up over the mountain. I'd be glad to escort you."

His voice was so casual that, for a moment, Hallie wondered if he was serious. She waited for him to say something else, but he remained silent.

He's only being insulting, she thought. She tried to come up with a smart answer that would put him in his place, but he turned and left the room before she could think of one.

ELEVEN

"What's wrong with Becky?" Adam asked Hallie that afternoon. "She was totally zoned out at lunch. And then I tried to get her to come for a walk with me, or at least go outside and throw a baseball—anything to pass the time—but she's always busy doing stuff with Mrs. Grigsby."

"What kind of stuff?" Hallie asked.

"Right now the two of them are in that little room off the back hall—the one with all the dried weeds. Who knows what they're up to?"

"Those aren't weeds. They're herbs, and that's Mrs. Grigsby's famous herb room. Listen, Adam, be patient with Becky. She's the only one of us who's enjoying her stay here. You know how hung up she is on history—this herb medicine thing is right up her alley. So what are you doing this afternoon?"

"What *is* there to do? Can you believe there isn't one movie theater or TV set in this entire town? There's not even a tennis court!"

"I thought you'd go back to watching Norman fix the van," Hallie said.

"Are you kidding? I'm afraid of him—he acts really weird when I'm there. I'll just hang out with you."

Hallie and Adam walked out to the Green, where the villagers were putting the finishing touches on their preparations for the festival. The old oak was hung with garlands. A group of men, under the direction of the vicar, were raking the Green, and the bonfire had been made ready. Logs and bones had been heaped high around the stake and platform. Hallie told Adam about the tradition of a bonefire and the burning of a straw maiden.

"Are you kidding me?" Adam asked. "They're really going to burn an effigy at the stake?"

"Yes. It's kind of a symbolic thing," said Hallie.

"Boy, these guys sure know how to throw a party," Adam said with a shudder. "Nothing like sacrificing a virgin to break the ice."

"I think it's bizarre," Hallie said.

"It's not my idea of a fun festival, that's for sure," Adam said.

Hallie moved a little closer to him and lowered her voice. "Listen, Adam, these people are fanatics. I went into their church this morning. All I wanted to do was look around, but the minister popped out of a back room and practically threw me out the door. You should see the inside of that church! I'll be so glad when we're out of here."

Adam groaned. "It's just my luck to get stuck in a town like this. Why couldn't we have been stranded in a cool place?"

"The church isn't the only weird thing," Hallie continued. "Look at those kids over there, Adam. Do they look healthy to you?"

"Not really. They look kind of pale and skinny."

"Have you noticed we've only seen a couple of children in this town?" Hallie asked. "No babies in strollers. No parents with toddlers."

"To tell you the truth, Hallie, I haven't given it much thought."

"Well, I have. You know how it is at home—you can't walk around the mall without tripping over strollers. So what's with these people?"

"I hope you're not going to make me ask them," Adam said.

Hallie grasped his arm and pulled him to a stop. "This isn't a joke, Adam. I'm dead serious. There's something really abnormal about this town."

"Because they don't have any kids running around?"

"Well, that and a lot of other stuff."

They started walking again. "Think about it, Adam," Hallie said. "Why is this place so isolated? There are lots of small towns and villages around, but they're not cut off from civilization like this, are they?"

Adam shook his head thoughtfully. "No."

"I think the people of Holyoake are cut off because they *want* to be cut off," Hallie said. "They don't need anyone else. Everybody here seems related to everybody else—it's like a clan. And they don't want to have anything to do with the twentieth century!"

They'd turned off onto the brick sidewalk that skirted the Green and were now nearing the church.

Hallie tugged on Adam's arm again. "Whatever you do, don't look like you're even *thinking* of going into that church. Did I tell you they have torches on the walls?"

Hallie didn't mention the marble font and its mysterious red stains. She was afraid Adam would think she'd gone overboard in her suspicions.

"Is that a graveyard behind the church?" Adam asked. "Let's go look. I love to read old tombstones. Some of them are really great."

"That's where the man came this morning," said Hallie. "He turned and ran back here."

"What man?"

"Didn't I tell you? Remember the man we met on the road—the one who told us how to get here?"

"Sure. Nice guy."

"Well, I saw him this morning, by the church," Hallie said, "and when he saw me, he got this funny look on his face and ran around the side of the church, like he was scared of me."

"You're kidding. Why would he be scared?"

"I don't know. It was really peculiar."

"Are you sure it was the same guy?" Adam asked.

"Absolutely." Hallie was silent for a moment and then asked, "Did he happen to tell you he was from Holyoake?"

"No. He acted like he didn't know much about the place, except that it had a gas station."

"That's the impression I got, too," Hallie said. "I'm sure he's from Holyoake, though. He looks like all the others."

"Then why didn't he say so at the time?" Adam asked.

"That's what I've been wondering," replied Hallie. "He sure didn't want me to see him this morning. It was like he didn't want me to know he lived here."

"You don't think he had some crazy reason for sending us here, do you, Hallie? Maybe he doesn't want you to know he's from here, because you might figure he set us up."

"Set us up for what?"

"Who knows?" Adam said darkly.

The old graveyard was shadowed and damp and ringed on all sides by tall pine trees. The ground was carpeted by fallen needles, and the teens' feet passed noiselessly over the spongy dirt.

The tombstones were of slate and stone, worn and disfigured by time. Some were tilted, others fallen, and the inscriptions on many of them were nearly indecipherable.

Hallie and Adam walked through the rows of graves, pausing from time to time to read what was carved on some of the newer ones. The same names came up, time after time, as if the number of original families had been small, with few new ones being added as the years progressed.

Finally Adam and Hallie found themselves at the far end of the graveyard.

"This is it, I guess," Adam said, looking around.

"I think there are some more graves over there," Hallie said.

A carefully pruned hedge of English boxwood fenced off a corner of the graveyard, creating an isolated enclosure. Hallie and Adam entered through a break in the hedge.

A group of white marble headstones, all uniform in height and width, stood in two neat, closely spaced rows. They appeared to be well tended.

Hallie went over to them, walking between the rows, and scanned the inscriptions.

"Look at this," she called to Adam. "All the tombstones are those of young girls. And they're all sixteen to eighteen years old. Some of them go back over two hundred years. See?"

Adam joined her and peered down at the stones. "Wait, Hallie. These aren't tombstones—they're memorial markers. Nobody's buried under these stones. They're set too close together to be graves."

Hallie looked around her. Each stone was

spaced only a couple of feet from its neighbor, far enough apart only to accommodate the planting of a few flowers between them.

"I think you're right," she said slowly. "And for some reason, this section gets a lot of care. See where they've mulched all around the flowers?"

Adam knelt and studied the markers. "Did you see the dates on the stones?" he asked. His voice was tight and strained. "They all died on the first of May. Different years, but always on the first of May."

"The first of May. May Day . . . Beltane," Hallie said, feeling as if a cold hand had just taken hold of her heart.

"Beltane." Adam's face was pale. "They all died on Beltane, from Lucinda Stockwell in 1704 to Deborah Evans ten years ago. She's the latest one."

Hallie got down on her knees beside Adam and took a closer look at the inscriptions.

"That's not all, Adam," she said. "They've all got the same picture carved on them. See? There on the base of each one."

The engraved image was a picture of crossed bones surmounted by flames.

"What is it?" Adam asked. "Is it supposed to be a bonfire?"

"No," Hallie said, almost in a whisper. "It's a *bonefire.*"

Bonefire. Bonfire. May the first. All this—the memorials, the dead girls—has something to do with the odd religion no one wants to talk about, Hallie thought with a deadly certainty. *The religion that got these people cast out of England, these people with their church Outsiders aren't supposed to see. Bonefire. Bonfire. May the first.*

"Wait a minute!" Adam was saying. "I've seen that bonfire picture before! Norman has a tattoo like that on his wrist. I saw it when he was working on the van. Crossbones and a flame. Just like the inscription on these stones."

Hallie gasped, remembering. "And so does Reverend Thoreson! I remember seeing what looked like a small tattoo on his wrist, but he saw me looking and pulled down his cuff."

"On his wrist? Right. That's where Norman's was."

"I didn't want to stare at the reverend's," Hallie continued. "It seemed so strange, him being a minister and all, and then having this tattoo—"

"But was it the same one?" Adam interrupted.

"I can't swear to it, but I think it was. I remember seeing what looked like a flame. Oh, Adam, what does all this mean?"

"I don't know, Hallie, but I'm starting to get scared. I'll be glad when we can get the heck out of this miserable town."

They stared at each other, eyes wide. Neither heard the footsteps that came toward them across the soft earth of the cemetery.

Hallie was suddenly aware of long legs in faded jeans standing beside her, and a lean, muscular arm reaching down to help her to her feet.

An arm that bore the bonefire sign tattooed on its wrist.

"Simon!" Hallie gasped. "What are you doing here?"

"I live here, remember? And we all take turns doing odd jobs around the churchyard on Saturdays."

He cocked his head at her quizzically, as if to ask her what *she*—and Adam—were doing here.

He was still holding her wrist, but gently this time, not the way he had last night. Hallie wondered if he could feel her pulse and if he'd noticed how rapidly it was beating. Would he think she was nervous because of *him*?

The thought angered Hallie. Why was he always following her around, anyway?

"I suppose you're wondering what we're doing here," she said heatedly. "I mean, Outsiders in

Holyoake are obviously not encouraged to go anywhere or look at anything."

Simon only shrugged, his face inscrutable.

"I'm sorry you find the people of Holyoake so inhospitable, Hallie," he said. "Actually Aunt Phoebe asked me to find you and tell you that dinner will be a little early tonight. She's got a meeting at the church afterwards. Some emergency's come up regarding the Beltane festival."

He turned on his heel and walked off.

"When they invented the word *cool*," Adam said, looking at Simon's erect, retreating back, "they must have had that guy in mind."

TWELVE

"You followed her and the boy this afternoon, as instructed, and they went where?" asks Reverend Thorcson.

"Just out on the Green," answers Simon. "Then to the old cemetery."

"The cemetery? What part of the cemetery?"

Simon shifts uneasily from one foot to the other. The vicar has not given him permission to sit. "They were just . . . uh . . . walking around when I caught up with them."

"They weren't over by the memorials to the Fire Maidens?"

Simon looks directly into the vicar's eyes. "No."

"Good," says the vicar. "That makes our job a little easier."

"Sir?"

"She and that boy might have put two and two together if they saw the markers. We couldn't risk that, not now. We would have had to eradicate them now, instead of later."

The vicar leans forward in his chair. "What a nuisance that would have been, with everyone so busy with the festival! Besides, it could have caused difficulties with Becky. One never can safely predict the behavior of young girls, can one?"

"No, I guess not."

"And you are prepared for what you must do when the festival is over?"

"Yes, sir."

"You are to dispose of the girl. Just the girl. Someone else can handle the boy. He might prove a little stronger, and since this is your first . . ."

"Yes, sir. I understand."

The vicar fixes his strange, silvery-gray gaze on Simon. "I hope you realize what an honor it is we are bestowing on you. A leap of faith, as it were, and a show of trust."

"Yes. I'm very grateful."

"This is your chance, Simon, to make up for past offenses against The Goddess. Offenses you inherited in your tainted bloodline."

Simon's jaw tightens slightly, and a muscle in his cheek twitches, but the vicar doesn't notice.

"Yes, my boy. If you do this job well, you can, at last, truly be one of us—a loyal son of The Goddess."

"You can depend on me to do the right thing," Simon replies.

THIRTEEN

Something was very, very wrong with Becky.

When Hallie and Adam returned to Mrs. Grigsby's, they found their friend staring at the living room wall, distant and wide-eyed.

When they tried to talk to her, she responded pleasantly, but vacantly, in one-syllable words.

"Are you okay, Becky?" Hallie asked anxiously. "Is something wrong?"

Just then a smiling and rosy Mrs. Grigsby appeared in the doorway, taking Becky's attention away from her friends. Frustrated, Hallie couldn't help feeling that her landlady's sweet-little-old-lady act was just that. An act.

"Oh, Becky," Mrs. Grigsby said with a smile.

"You said you wanted to watch me prepare the spinach soufflé for supper."

She smiled apologetically at Hallie and Adam. "I'm usually a meat and potatoes cook, but I do make a lovely soufflé. Becky said she'd like to learn how it's done."

Without a word, Becky rose from her chair and followed Mrs. Grigsby out of the room.

"Did you see that, Hallie?" Adam asked. "I'm worried. I mean, really worried. Becky was zoning at lunch, but this is ridiculous! What does she care about a stupid soufflé? She's acting like a zombie! If I didn't know her better, I'd think she was on something."

"I know, and it scares me, too," Hallie admitted. "Talking to her was like talking to a wall. No response."

"I saw it," Adam agreed, "and I don't know what to think. The only person she seems to listen to is Mrs. Grigsby. You don't think she's hypnotized Becky or anything, do you?"

Then he smiled and made a helpless gesture with his hands. "That sounds crazy, doesn't it? I just can't figure out what's going on with Becky."

"Everything I've been thinking since we came to Holyoake would sound crazy if I said it aloud,"

Hallie told him. "But the time has come to say it, no matter how far out it sounds."

She glanced quickly over her shoulder to make sure Mrs. Grigsby wasn't lurking in the shadows. Then she took Adam's hands in hers, drew him over to the sofa, and sat down with him before the cold and empty fireplace. A slight wind in the chimney rattled the embers on the hearth.

"Listen, Adam. We've got to get out of this place. And soon," she said. "I think Becky needs help."

"I know. I realized that when we came in here this afternoon. But how are we going to do it? We can't go anywhere until we get the van fixed, and the new fuel pump won't get here until Tuesday morning."

Hallie groaned. "This is a nightmare. Tuesday is three days away. What are we going to do in the meantime?"

A terrible thought struck her. "Adam . . . you don't think Norman is lying about the van, do you? I mean, about it needing a new fuel pump?"

"Why would he do that?"

Something about Adam's voice told Hallie that the thought had crossed his mind, too.

"Didn't you say the man who sold you the van said the fuel pump was brand new?"

111

"Yes," Adam said. "I thought he was a pretty straight guy, too. But how could it have gone bad so soon, unless . . . ?"

"Unless it *didn't* go bad," Hallie finished for him.

Adam looked at her grimly. "Those holes in the hoses, too. Hallie, those hoses were brand new—I had a couple of them put in a month ago. And I'm willing to swear they were okay when we first got here. I'd have noticed something was wrong with them all those times along the way when I checked the motor. What could have happened to them? I can't believe that somebody—Norman—would punch holes in them. Do you think maybe they were faulty, and I just didn't notice?"

"No. I don't know anything about cars, but I can't remember seeing holes or anything leaking from those hoses, either," Hallie told him. "Remember that last time we stopped? Before we came to the turnoff to Holyoake? I was watching over your shoulder when you were banging on the motor. If those hoses had holes in them, surely one of us would have noticed, wouldn't we?"

"But why?" asked Adam. "What would be the purpose of doing something like that?"

112

"I don't know," Hallie admitted.

Adam took a deep breath. "He sure seems eager to convince me—us—that everything under the hood is in bad shape, though. Do you think he's been lying all along?"

"Maybe. But if he's trying to keep us here for some reason, why did he send Miss Netty to make a call for us? Surely he must have realized that Mr. Costello—and our folks—might come here to help us, once they found out where we were," Hallie said.

Adam hesitated, then finally said, "That's another thing that worries me. How do we know he really got that message to our folks? I mean, we only have his word on it, the same way we have his word about the fuel pump. And the hoses."

Hallie felt her blood run cold.

"Why would he do that, Adam? What possible motive could he have? He must know we'll find out the truth when the phone lines are repaired."

Adam's forehead puckered. "I don't know, Hallie. This place is weird, and getting weirder. The fact is, those phone lines aren't getting fixed. And what's the big problem with them, anyway? The lines go down during storms at home, and the repair people get right out there and fix them within hours."

"You're right," Hallie agreed. "I haven't even seen any repair workers. . . . Well, there *was* one this morning, but he disappeared right away. And I really couldn't tell if he was fixing the lines or disconnecting them. It was weird."

She looked over her shoulder again, to make sure Mrs. Grigsby or Simon hadn't come up undetected. But the foyer was empty. From out in the kitchen Hallie could hear voices. Mrs. Grigsby's, high and lilting. Becky's, a dull monotone.

"I'm scared, Adam," she whispered. "I haven't wanted to admit it to myself until now, but I'm scared."

She paused, waiting for Adam to tell her she was being silly or overly imaginative. Instead, he looked at her soberly.

"That church," she told him. "It isn't like any church I've ever seen. It looks like something out of an old witchcraft movie. I mean, thirteen chairs around that black table, Adam, like a witches' coven!"

Adam nodded. "I felt that way about those stone markers. All those young girls, and every last one of them died on May first."

"Beltane," Hallie said slowly. "And the bonfire. Every stone marker had the engraving of a bonfire on it. And then the tattoos. Norman's. Simon's. Reverend Thoreson's. I wonder how many other people in Holyoake have them."

Adam looked at her strangely. He opened his mouth as if to say something, then shut it.

"What is it, Adam?" Hallie demanded. "We can't keep any secrets now."

"Okay, then," Adam said. "I'll say it." He looked down at his hands. Hallie could see they were trembling slightly. "There's at least one other tattoo around here that I know of."

"What do you mean?"

"Didn't you see it?"

Hallie shook her head, bewildered.

"Mrs. Grigsby has one. Just like Norm's and Simon's. One with bones and a flame."

FOURTEEN

The spinach soufflé that night was delicious. So was the pork roast and the oven-browned potatoes. It was the company that turned everything sour.

Mrs. Grigsby was at her finest—blue eyes sparkling, little white curls dancing, talking way too much. *Is this an effort to keep us from noticing the way Becky's acting?* Hallie wondered. Becky sat there like a ghost, staring straight ahead of her, answering questions in an awful, monotone voice.

Adam stared at his plate, his freckles dark against his pale face. Adam, who usually never worried, never really saw anything to worry about. Who'd never looked pale in all the years Hallie had known him.

Simon sat at his end of the table, aloof and silent, his head bowed. Hallie couldn't help noticing his meticulous table manners—the deft, almost surgical way his long fingers cut his meat. The way he held his fork. His quick and efficient way of eating. Surely he must have felt the tension that hung like a thick black cloud over the dinner table.

Every now and then he'd pause and glance up at Mrs. Grigsby, his dark eyes unreadable.

Long ago Hallie had decided that dark eyes were more unreadable than light eyes. There was something masked about dark eyes—you couldn't see into them. But looking into light eyes was like looking into a lake. You could always see what was swimming around beneath the surface.

But Hallie realized now that she'd been wrong. Mrs. Grigsby's blue eyes, open and sparkling, hid what she was thinking as effectively as a visor. Everything about Mrs. Grigsby, including her innocent wide eyes, was a fake.

At the end of the meal, Mrs. Grigsby picked up her spoon and tapped playfully on her water glass. "Are you all paying attention? Becky has some good news."

Hallie felt her stomach tighten. "What kind of good news?" she asked suspiciously.

"Tell them, Becky dear," prompted Mrs. Grigsby.

Becky only stared at her blankly, so Mrs. Grigsby said, gently reproving, "You know, dear. About the festival."

When Becky spoke, her smile was vacant and her voice flat and emotionless. "I've been picked to be the May Queen at the Beltane festival."

Mrs. Grigsby smiled broadly. "Isn't that wonderful, children?"

Hallie stared at Becky in dismay. *Nothing,* she thought, *is as scary as Becky is right now. She's like a puppet.*

"What do you mean, May Queen?" asked Adam.

Becky only smiled.

"Why, the one who presides over all the festival activities, of course," said Mrs. Grigsby, answering for Becky. "It's a real honor. And her an Outsider, too."

"But why Becky?" Hallie asked through tight lips. *May Queen for that awful reenactment of the good old days when they burned maidens at the stake?*

"The girl who was supposed to be this year's

119

Queen got sick," Mrs. Grigsby explained. "And Becky's such a pretty girl, with all that lovely long red hair. At a special festival-committee meeting this morning, we unanimously voted to have her as our Queen. Isn't that lovely?"

After dinner, when Mrs. Grigsby was in the kitchen cleaning up, and Simon had pulled yet another of his disappearing acts, Adam and Hallie took Becky aside.

"Listen to me, Becky," Hallie said, taking her friend by the shoulders and shaking her gently. "What's happening to you? You're acting so funny. Are you on something?"

Becky only looked at her, innocent and wide-eyed. *Just like Mrs. Grigsby*, Hallie thought.

"Why, Hallie," Becky said in the monotone voice Hallie had come to hate. "Nothing's the matter. Holyoake is such a lovely place. Being May Queen at the festival is a real honor. Now, if you will excuse me, I'm going out to help Aunt Phoebe."

"Aunt Phoebe?" Hallie repeated when Becky had left the room.

"Do you remember that old movie *The Stepford Wives*, Hallie?" Adam asked. "We saw it last year at the film festival. You know, about that town where the men all turn their wives into robots?"

Hallie nodded.

"Well," Adam said, "do you suppose there really *is* a way of doing something like that?"

Adam was so serious, so intense, that Hallie's first impulse was to laugh. Adam, who didn't believe in anything that couldn't be explained by common sense. And then she thought, *If Adam's scared enough to think Becky's been turned into a robot, then we've really got something to worry about.*

"No," she said thoughtfully. "I don't think it's as far out as that. I think Becky's on something."

"Becky? She refuses to even look at cigarette ads!" Adam said.

"I think it's those herb teas Mrs. Grigsby's been giving her. Who knows what's in them?"

Hallie put her hand on Adam's shoulder. "That must be it! Did you see her eyes? They're glassy, and her pupils are enlarged. But why is Mrs. Grigsby doing this?"

"God, Hallie, I don't know. I'd give anything to be a million miles away from this crummy place."

"We've got to keep Becky away from Mrs. Grigsby," Hallie said. "How dumb can we get?

We keep leaving her alone with that woman. I'm going in there right now and get Becky away."

Hallie managed to drag Becky upstairs, but Becky wasn't able to get ready for bed by herself. She waited patiently for Hallie to find her nightie and help her into it.

As Hallie gently removed Becky's sweater, she saw something around her friend's neck that made her feel dizzy and faint.

A bronze amulet. An amulet with an engraved picture of a bonfire on it.

Just like the tattoo on Simon's wrist. And Norman's. And Mrs. Grigsby's.

"Becky! Becky!" Hallie said, trying to rouse her friend from her torpor. "Where did you get this?"

She held the amulet on its long cord up before Becky's eyes. Becky only looked at it silently, blankly.

"Look, Becky," Hallie said desperately. "This . . . thing . . . you're wearing around your neck. See?"

Becky finally blinked and looked at the amulet with mild curiosity. She smiled faintly. "Pretty," she said.

"But where did you get it?" Hallie demanded, trying to keep her voice calm. "Think,

Becky! Did Mrs. Grigsby give it to you?"

Becky puckered her forehead. "I don't know," she finally replied, and no amount of questioning could make her remember.

After she'd put Becky to bed, Hallie paced the floor in a frenzy of nerves, wanting desperately to tell Adam about the amulet. She walked over to the window and looked out, listening to Becky's deep and even breathing. Becky always slept soundly—she wouldn't wake up for hours. It was safe now to go to Adam.

Just then a flicker of light on the far side of the Green caught her eye. There it was again, just like last night. Torches. The villagers were gathering again. *Why?* Hallie thought. *Why do they keep meeting like this? What do they do in that old church?*

And does it have something to do with Becky?

FIFTEEN

Hallie remained frozen at the window.

What are they doing? she asked herself again. Should Adam and she try to go over there and spy on them? Would they get caught?

And would Simon be the one to catch them?

Simon. She thought about him for a moment. What was it with him and his aunt? What did those looks he was giving her tonight mean? Mrs. Grigsby showed her disapproval of him in a hundred little ways. And Norman seemed to outright dislike him. Was there some secret about Simon? Is that what made him so hostile?

Hallie looked at the church again and made her decision. She'd better go to Adam right now.

Something terrible was happening over there, and the sooner they found out what it was, the better.

The mental picture of the marble font with its blood-colored stains flashed before her eyes. Hallie shook her head to clear the thought. Closing the door softly behind her, she tiptoed over to Adam's room and scratched lightly at his door.

To her surprise he answered immediately. He was still dressed in jeans, sweatshirt, and running shoes.

"I'm glad you came, Hallie," he said. "I've been thinking about everything we saw today— I'm too wound up to go to bed."

"Remember what I told you about last night? About how all those people were in the church, dressed in white robes and carrying torches?" Hallie said.

Adam nodded.

"Well," she went on breathlessly, "they're at it again. I saw them from my window, and I'm scared, Adam. I have this terrible feeling that what they're doing has something to do with us."

"You wait here, Hallie, and I'll sneak over and take a look."

"No! I want to go with you."

"What about Becky?" Adam asked. "Will she be okay?"

"She's fast asleep," Hallie replied. "Come on, Adam. We're only wasting time."

Adam picked up a small flashlight from his nightstand, and together they left the room and slipped quietly down the steps.

There was no one waiting at the bottom of the stairs, no one looming up suddenly from the darkness to stop them. Hallie released the anxious breath she'd been holding.

"I hope the front door doesn't squeak," Adam whispered.

He carefully turned the handle and opened the door . . . slowly.

And came face-to-face with Simon.

Simon was standing on the front porch. Hallie could see his face clearly in the light from the full moon. She caught her breath in surprise—this was an altogether different Simon. The black, glowering look was gone. His face was pale and anxious. He even looked younger, Hallie noticed. Younger and more vulnerable.

And scared.

Simon cast a quick look over his shoulder and shoved Hallie and Adam back into the hall.

"Shhh," he cautioned, his finger on his lips. "Get back inside. Quick!"

"What are you doing here?" Hallie whispered indignantly.

"Don't start with me, Hallie," Simon said. "We don't have time. I'm on your side."

"On our side?" Hallie's voice rose to a squeak. "Since when?"

He put his hand over her mouth. This time it was gentle, a warning that she was making too much noise.

"Aunt Phoebe is over at the church," he explained in a low voice. "I was supposed to keep an eye on the three of you. We only have an hour, and we need to talk."

He removed his hand from her mouth. "Where's the best place, Adam's room?"

Hallie nodded.

Adam led the way upstairs. Simon brought up the rear, still casting anxious glances over his shoulder. Hallie glanced in at Becky, who was sleeping soundly.

"Wait, don't turn on the light yet," Simon cautioned.

He went over to the window and closed the blinds while Hallie and Adam perched apprehensively on the edge of the bed. Then he snapped on the night-light that stood on the bureau.

"You've got to get out of town," he said. "Tonight."

"Tonight?" Adam repeated. "Why?"

Simon glanced at the window, then moved to the center of the room. Hallie wondered if he was afraid his shadow would show on the blind.

Is someone out there, watching?

"Maybe I ought to explain the situation you've blundered into," Simon told them. "It sounds crazy, but you've got to believe me if you want to get out of Holyoake alive."

Alive? Hallie's mouth went dry and she began to tremble. So she'd been right all along—there *was* some terrible secret concerning Holyoake!

Adam tensed. "Get out alive?" he asked quietly. "It sounds like you've got some real explaining to do."

Simon nodded. "I'll try to make it brief."

He pulled out the desk chair and straddled it. "It's true what Aunt Phoebe told you—about how the earliest settlers came here so they could practice their religion in peace," he began. "But what she didn't tell you was that their religion was a primitive form of paganism, a holdover from earliest times. And that they believed—and still believe today—in human sacrifice."

"Human sacrifice!" Adam gasped.

Hallie put her hands to her mouth. "This can't be true," she whispered.

"It *is* true. And I'm sure you believe me, even if you don't want to admit it to yourself."

"What kind of human sacrifice?" Adam said. "That stake out on the Green, in the middle of the bonfire . . . that doesn't . . . I mean, they're going to burn a straw figure, they said."

"Do you really think they're going to come right out and tell you their plans?" Simon said. "They intend to use Becky as the Beltane sacrifice!"

"Becky? But—" Hallie began.

"You're crazy!" Adam blurted out.

Simon raised his hands to silence them.

"Look," he said. "We don't have time for all this. Aunt Phoebe might come home early, and we've got some planning to do. There's a way out of this mess, and that's what I want to talk to you about."

"But—" Adam said.

"I think you must realize I'm telling the truth," Simon interrupted. "You saw those memorial stones in the graveyard. And the platform. And the stake."

He paused for a moment, then added grimly, "After tomorrow, there's going to be another stone in the graveyard."

Hallie's lips were so stiff with horror, she could scarcely force the next words out. "One with . . . *Becky's* name on it?"

"Yes." Simon's voice was low. "They're going to kill Becky."

Adam's face twisted in agony. "This can't be happening. I must be having a nightmare!"

"I wish you were," Simon told him. "But you're not. Surely you've suspected that there's something terribly wrong with this town and its people."

He turned to Hallie. "You knew there was something funny going on with the phones—you even caught me using one. You could have called out that first night. But now the lines are truly disconnected, so you can't get help from the outside world."

Adam was obviously still in shock. "And Miss Netty?" His voice was flat. Emotionless. "The one who was supposed to call our teacher. That was all a lie, too?"

"Yes," Simon said. "Norman pulled a fast one about getting in touch with your people, just as he did about fixing the van. He could have repaired it right away, and you could have been out of here. But then he saw Becky. The whole village did."

"But why Becky?" Hallie asked.

"Because physically she's the perfect traditional Fire Maiden," Simon explained. "Hair the color of flame. That's the main requirement. The Fire Maidens all had red hair, and that's a pretty rare color hereabouts. But Reverend Thoreson sent out scouts, and one of them, Brother William, met up with you on the road and sent you here."

"You mean it was a setup?" Adam asked brokenly. "We thought everybody was helping us. Becky thought they were all so wonderful." He passed a hand over his eyes. "And all along they've been planning to . . ."

"Yes. The villagers took your arrival as an answer to their prayers. They thought The Goddess had personally sent Becky to be their Beltane sacrifice."

"The Goddess?" Hallie asked.

"My ancestors have been worshiping her since the beginning of time," Simon explained. "But that's not important. What matters is that you've got to get out of here before tomorrow morning, when the festival begins."

The thought of positive action, something they could do to save Becky, put the fighting spirit back in Hallie. Adam, too, from what she could see.

Adam sat upright and rubbed his hands together. "If the van's okay, then all we have to do is sneak over there and—"

"Forget that," Simon told him. "Norman's scrapped the insides. And the few cars we have in Holyoake are under lock and key. Besides Norman, only the vicar and the elders are allowed to own cars."

He leaned forward, his eyes dark and intense. "This village is like a prison. To try to leave, or to betray our secrets, brings an automatic death sentence. You're going to have to escape on foot, over the mountain. It's a risk, but there's no other way."

"Wait a minute," Hallie said suspiciously. "Why are you doing this? How do we know you're not putting us on, the way everyone else has ever since we came to this godforsaken hole?"

"Because I'm not one of them," Simon explained.

He stood up and moved restlessly about the room, keeping his distance from the windows.

"The last sacrifice of a Fire Maiden was ten

years ago," he said. "My parents had begun to disapprove of the old ways. My mother was an Outsider, and the village religion horrified her."

Simon's eyes grew distant as he spoke.

"I was only seven years old. I didn't see the sacrifice. My parents made me stay in my room. And later that night I heard them talking. They wanted to get away from Holyoake and start again. So the three of us attempted to escape. We were supposed to go over the mountains, the same route you'll be taking tonight."

"If you and your folks didn't make it, what makes you think we will?" Adam asked.

Simon's face twisted. "We might have made it, but we were betrayed . . . by Aunt Phoebe. She inherited the house when my parents were executed."

"Executed!" Hallie gasped.

"Yes. Stoned to death, just like in olden times. And by my parents' neighbors and supposed friends."

"How could they? How could anyone do that?" Hallie asked.

"Because my parents were traitors by Holyoake standards. And I would have been executed, too, if Reverend Thoreson hadn't stepped in. He gave me to Aunt Phoebe to raise—against her will, of course. She, as well as everyone else in the village, has always held my parents' 'treachery' against me."

"I didn't realize Reverend Thoreson was so generous," Hallie said sourly. "I mean, to save your life like that."

"He had some idea he could bring me back into the fold," Simon said. "And when you three wandered in, and they saw Becky, the vicar thought this was a good chance for me to prove my loyalty."

"What made you change your mind about letting Becky die?" Hallie put in.

"I never intended to let her die," Simon said. "I wanted to help, but I didn't know how."

"Well, you could have fooled me," Hallie said, "especially that first night, when you kept me from going into the church. And that business about the phone. You acted like one of *them*."

"I had to act that way. I wanted them to think I was eager to do my duty to Holyoake. Besides, Hallie, I wanted to see what you were like before I told you anything."

Simon turned to Adam. "And you, Adam—I didn't know how reliable you were, either. I had to wait and see what you were like."

"You've never told us what's supposed to be

done with Hallie and me if they . . . you know . . . to Becky," Adam said slowly.

Simon looked down at his hands.

"I'm supposed to kill Hallie," he said. "And one of the elders will dispose of you, Adam."

He cleared his throat, still looking down.

"And it's supposed to happen tomorrow afternoon, right after the festival. After Becky's been burned at the stake."

SIXTEEN

After Becky is burned at the stake.

Putting it into words—*burned at the stake*—made it seem so real. So final.

No, not final. Hallie would not allow these insane people, locked in their brutal time warp, to do this terrible thing to her friend. Becky, tied to a stake and . . . No. Never!

Adam stood up. His face was pale, but his jaw was set.

"Nobody's going to do that to Becky," he told Simon. "We'll leave as soon as we can by that mountain road. Holyoake's not going to have its Fire Maiden this year. Tell us what we should do to get out of here, Simon."

"Okay," said Simon. "I've given it a lot of thought, and here's my plan."

The three teens leaned closer toward one another, their heads nearly touching.

"When Aunt Phoebe comes back from church, I'll suggest she check on you, to make sure you're all in bed and asleep," Simon told them. "Then I'll go off to my room. This will put me in the clear and give me an alibi when you turn up missing."

He looked at Hallie and smiled. It was the first time she'd seen him smile, and a small corner of her mind registered the fact that he looked pretty cute when he did.

"As you've noticed, Hallie," he said, "I've taken a lot of pains to make people, including you, think I dislike the three of you intensely. And I've convinced the vicar and the elders that I'm eager to perform my duties in the sacrifice so that I can finally be worthy of a position of honor and authority in the community."

"By killing me?" Hallie murmured incredulously. "That's honor?"

"Around here it is," Simon said.

"You mean you aren't coming with us?" Adam asked. "You've got to get out of this place, too."

"No. It's better I stay here and try to cover

your escape. But if—when—you make it, go to the police, the FBI, the newspapers, whatever, and tell them what's going on here. I'll be waiting. And I've got plenty to tell them."

"Why haven't you ever tried to escape, Simon?" Hallie asked.

"Who would believe a runaway teen with a crazy story like this? I'm underage. They'd probably only return me to my devoted aunt. But now I've got three witnesses to back me up. They're bound to believe me now."

Simon pulled a small notebook and a pencil from his back pocket.

"Now here's the route," he said, sketching. "The worst part is getting past the Green and Norman's store. Once you're beyond that, though, you go off the road right here—" he indicated a spot on the map "—and go into the woods."

He looked up and added, "Those woods are thick and full of brambles and fallen tree limbs. Even with a full moon, you won't be able to see much. Your flashlight will be a little help, but you'll have to go slowly and watch where you put your feet."

Simon returned to the map. "Now right about here is a stream. You'll probably hear it before you see it. Follow it upstream, and it will curve around and cross the road you entered Holyoake on, but to the west of the mountain road. It's safer if you avoid that intersection anyway."

"Okay. I know what you mean. Then what?" Adam asked tensely.

"Once you cross the road, you'll keep following the stream until you get to this trail." Again he indicated the spot on his map. "The trail goes up over the mountains. It will be a long walk, but you'll eventually come to a town. A safe one, with a police station."

"So when do you think we should leave?" Adam asked. He sounded a bit breathless. Hallie knew he was as nervous as she was.

"Wait until after midnight," Simon replied. "After Aunt Phoebe looks in on you, she'll go to bed. She sleeps like a log, and she's a little deaf, although she won't admit it, so she won't hear you as long as you're quiet in the hall and on the stairs. Now, as you know, the front door bolts from within, so you won't need a key to open it. I oiled the bolt this afternoon, so it will slide easily and quietly."

Hallie marveled at the way Simon had thought of everything.

"Keep to the right side when you go down the

outside steps. There's a bush on that side, so stay in its shadows. And do the same when you're out on the street. There are plenty of trees and bushes to hide you as you head out of town."

He looked at his watch. "We'd better break up now. The church meeting will be ending soon."

"Then I—we—won't be seeing you until this is all over," Hallie said, her voice breaking.

She reached over and took his hand. It was warm and steady. "Thank you, Simon. For everything."

He laid his other hand over hers. "I'll be waiting for you to return with the law. Don't forget me, Hallie."

"I couldn't forget you," she said. "Ever."

Hallie went to bed fully clothed, including her sneakers. She would have liked to get Becky dressed, too, but that would involve waking her, and Hallie wanted to be sure Becky was asleep when Mrs. Grigsby did her bed check.

When she heard Mrs. Grigsby coming down the hall, Hallie pulled the covers up under her chin and closed her eyes.

The door creaked open, and Hallie could hear Mrs. Grigsby's heavy breathing as she stood there, peering in. Finally the door closed, and after a moment she heard Adam's door being opened. Another moment passed. Then the sound of Adam's door closing and Mrs. Grigsby's footsteps receding down the hall in the direction of her room.

Hallie was trembling when the old clock on the landing struck midnight. She'd never been so frightened in her life.

I've got to think positively, Hallie told herself fiercely. *We're going to make it. We're all in good shape. We'll be miles away, over the mountains and safe in some police station, before anybody here even realizes we're gone.*

Getting Becky roused and dressed was a problem.

"Geez, Becky, haven't you slept off *any* of whatever it was Mrs. Grigsby gave you?" she muttered as she pulled a sweatshirt over Becky's head and forced her limp arms into the sleeves.

Becky only smiled cheerfully.

"Good morning, Hallie," she said. "Did you sleep well?"

When Becky was dressed, Hallie pulled her to her feet, fearful that Becky would fall down. The thought of her and Adam having to carry Becky out of town and over the mountain trail made her weak with fear. This was something they hadn't considered. They might not make it if Becky couldn't walk.

But once on her feet, Becky seemed steady and willing to walk. The only problem was making her keep her mouth shut. For some reason Becky wanted to sing the theme song from *Mr. Rogers' Neighborhood.*

"Listen, Becky," Hallie said, clapping her hand over Becky's mouth. "We've got to be quiet. Really quiet. Mrs. Grigsby isn't . . . uh . . . feeling well, and we don't want to wake her up. Okay?"

Becky nodded, her eyes huge as they peered over the edge of Hallie's hand. When Hallie released her, Becky whispered, "I'll be as quiet as a mouse. We mustn't wake up Aunt Phoebe."

Adam tapped gently at their door. "Are you ready?"

"Remember, Becky," Hallie cautioned, "be very quiet."

Becky smiled and put her finger to her lips.

The three crept cautiously down the hall. Hallie's heart was beating so loudly that she was sure *she'd* be the one to wake up Mrs. Grigsby.

They turned on the landing and were preparing to go down the stairs when Becky stopped.

"Wait," she said in a stage whisper. "I forgot something."

Hallie stifled a groan. "What?"

"My pretty necklace. Mrs. Grigsby said I was supposed to wear it everywhere."

"We'll get it later," Hallie told her.

"Is Becky okay?" Adam asked in a voice that was barely audible.

Hallie knew Adam was trembling. She could hear it in his uneven breathing.

"Yes. She's fine," Hallie assured him in a voice as low as his own.

Simon had done a good job oiling the large brass bolt on the front door. It opened smoothly and silently.

Following his instructions, the teens kept to the right on the porch stairs, then clung to the shadows of the trees and hedges that bordered the street as they headed back the way they'd come yesterday afternoon. Hallie couldn't believe it had been only yesterday. It seemed as if years had passed since they'd limped into town, pushing that treacherous, broken-down van.

They walked in single file, with Hallie leading, Becky in the middle, and Adam bringing up the rear. They were reaching the far end of the Green now. Norman's store and garage lay just ahead. A feeble light burned over the main counter. Hallie could see the jars of candy and the old-fashioned cash register, even from this distance. How innocent and charming it looked, she noted bitterly. The pleasant little village store by moonlight.

Now they'd reached the little road that dead-ended into Holyoake. They had to turn left here to head out of town. Hallie wondered if Norman lived over his store. And if he did, could he see them? She looked up. Sure enough, there were curtained windows on the second floor. She noted with relief that the curtains were closed, though, and nothing was moving behind them.

Again she told herself that they would come out of this okay. Before they knew it, they'd be on that mountain trail Simon had told them about, and they'd be safe from all the wild-eyed Holyoake crazies with their disgusting sacrifices.

And then it happened.

Adam was in the lead as they headed out of town. They'd gone about a quarter of a mile when he stopped so abruptly that the three of them collided into one another.

"Quick, over here," Adam whispered, pulling them behind a clump of trees that bordered the roadside.

Hallie drew Becky to her and peered out around the tree. "What is it?" she asked Adam.

"Up there, see?" he whispered.

A short distance ahead, in the center of the road, was a crude barricade. Two men carrying shotguns stood beside it. Fortunately they were facing the other way.

Hallie leaned close to Adam and said in a low voice, "Do you think they're trying to keep people out or in?"

"Probably both," Adam responded grimly. "They don't want Outsiders seeing what they're planning to do tomorrow. And they might be making sure we don't make a run for it, too."

"So what are we going to do?" Hallie asked desperately. "How are we going to get around them?"

"We'll have to leave the road sooner than the map indicates," Adam said. "We'll go through the woods, trying to keep as close as we can to the road, until we come to the place where we're supposed to run into the stream. We can't use the flashlight, though, and we're going to have to walk quietly."

Just then, one of the men turned, struck a match on the sole of his shoe, and lit his pipe. As the match flamed next to his face, they could see him perfectly. It was Elder Sidlaw.

"Oh, look!" Becky said in the clear, high-pitched robot's voice that Hallie had come to hate. "It's Mrs. Grigsby's friend, that nice Elder Sidlaw. I wonder what he's doing out there on the road."

Before either Hallie or Adam could grab her, Becky had stepped out from behind the cover of the trees.

"Good evening, Elder Sidlaw!" she called pleasantly, and waved to him.

SEVENTEEN

"Becky!" Hallie hissed, but it was too late. The men were looking their way.

"Oh, God, Becky!" Adam moaned. "You've done it. We're dead!"

Becky didn't seem to hear him. Avoiding his grasp, she moved forward a few paces into a patch of moonlight. Its rays haloed her hair, turning it to burnished copper.

"It's me—Becky!" she called out politely, waving again. "My friends and I are taking a nice walk."

What happened next was like something out of a nightmare, in which everything happened in slow motion. Hallie, watching, felt rooted to the ground, unable to move.

She saw Elder Sidlaw bend over and pick up something that was propped against the barricade. A rifle? No, maybe a shotgun. It was hard to tell at this distance and in the dark.

Adam made a strange sound in the back of his throat. Like an animal caught in a trap. For the moment, he seemed as incapable of movement as Hallie.

The other man turned abruptly and ran over to the shadows beside the road. Was that Brother William? There was something familiar about the way he stood and walked. Something about the way he held his head, chin down and hunched between his shoulders. And it looked like his Model T Ford parked behind the barricade.

Suddenly Hallie found herself staring into the twin beams of the old car's headlights.

She watched, wide eyed and trembling, as Elder Sidlaw, followed by Brother William, advanced toward them with leveled shotguns. They obviously meant business.

"Are they going to sh-shoot us, Adam?" Hallie could barely control the trembling of her voice.

"No. They're going to take us back to Holyoake," Adam said. "And that's even worse." Galvanized into sudden action by the thought,

Adam grabbed Hallie with one hand and Becky with the other. "Come on!"

He yanked them off the road and into the woods. "Come on! We've got to run for it!"

Once away from the lights of Brother William's Model T, Hallie felt as if she'd gone blind. The trees reached up and knitted their boughs together beneath the moon, allowing no light to shine through.

They plunged forward, the three of them, through the black velvet darkness, Adam in the lead. Hallie tripped over a fallen branch and fell down, but Adam jerked her to her feet again without even stopping. Unseen brambles tore at their clothing, and branches caught in their hair. Oddly enough, there was no sound of pursuit. No yelling by Elder Sidlaw and Brother William.

Hallie could hear Becky stumbling along behind, Adam dragging her, and the little sobbing breaths she was taking.

It isn't really Becky's fault we've been spotted, Hallie told herself. *She couldn't help herself. She's been hypnotized, or drugged, or something.*

At last, a little light trickled down through the interlaced branches. Enough light for Hallie to see Adam run into a thick branch that hung chest high and fall to the ground.

Hallie dropped to her knees beside him. "Adam! Are you all right?"

Just then they heard the boom of a gun. Three shots. A pause. Then three more shots. The sound came from behind them, on the road.

"What's that? What are they shooting at?"

"Oh, hell," Adam said, clutching his chest. "They're signaling those crazy villagers. Now they'll all be on our tails!"

"They'll have lanterns, too," Hallie said. "The whole village will be after us. We've got to get out of here. Now!"

"The stream," Adam said. "We've got to find the stream and follow it. It's our only chance."

"Do you remember the map?" Hallie asked. "Wasn't the stream around here somewhere?"

"Finding it in the dark will be like finding a needle in a haystack," said Adam. He rose to his feet. "Where's Becky?"

"She's over there by the tree," Hallie told him. "I don't know what's the matter with her now. She's kind of gone limp."

Adam groaned. "What next?"

Hallie tried to pull Becky to her feet, but her friend resisted. "You've got to walk, Becky. Won't you? For me?"

"No." Becky's voice sounded like that of someone under hypnosis. "I want to listen to the water."

Hallie crouched beside her and grabbed her shoulders. "Get up, Becky. Haven't you caused enough trouble for—What did you say? What water?"

The gun sounded again from the road. Three times. A pause. Then three more times.

"There they go again," Adam said. "Come on, let's move out while we can."

Hallie shook Becky—not hard, but Becky's head wobbled on her shoulders like a rag doll's.

"What water, Becky?"

"Over there," Becky responded dreamily. "Up ahead."

"Adam! Becky says the stream is up ahead!"

Rays of moonlight shone fitfully through the branches of the trees. In the far distance they could hear voices rising and falling.

"They've heard the shots. They know something's wrong," Hallie cried. "Come on, Becky, be a good girl. You've got to stand up and walk. Can you do that? Can you do that for Hallie?"

Becky didn't answer.

"Help me, Adam," Hallie begged.

The gun fired again. Three times. Pause. Repeat.

Together Adam and Hallie managed to drag Becky to her feet. Becky seemed to weigh a ton. She was deadweight. Hallie shuddered at the thought of the word *dead*. If they had to carry Becky, they'd never make it through the woods, stream or no stream.

"Listen to me, Becky," Hallie said desperately. "We're going to find the water and walk beside it. Won't that be nice?"

"Oh, all right," Becky said, suddenly agreeable and lively, as if she'd just been given a shot of adrenaline. She wriggled free of Hallie's hands. "Let's go find the nice water."

The herbs Mrs. Grigsby had fed Becky, Hallie reflected, seemed to work in spurts. First Becky would be lethargic. Then animated. If they could only keep her on her feet and moving until they got over the mountains!

Becky seemed to know where she was going, because she struck out immediately, rapidly, through the trees—surprisingly surefooted, in spite of the dark and the uneven terrain.

"Hurry up, Adam," Hallie urged. "We can't lose her."

They followed close behind, within touching distance of Becky, stepping carefully over the crackling underbrush and pushing aside overhanging branches. Sometimes they could see where they were going, sometimes not, but Becky seemed guided by an internal radar. She appeared able to hear the water, even though the others couldn't. Hallie wondered if the drug she was on had made her hearing supersensitive.

Then Hallie heard it, too. The sound of running water.

"She's done it, Adam! She's found the stream!"

They stepped out of the trees into a clearing. Unobstructed, the full moon shone down on the water that swirled and bubbled over dark rocks.

"Simon said to follow it upstream," Hallie said. "It will lead us to that trail over the mountains he told us about."

Adam cocked his head, listening. "Brother William's blowing his car horn. Hear it?"

"What does that mean?"

"He's probably letting everyone know where he is. That's smart. They'll start looking for us at the spot where we left the road. Then they'll all spread out into the woods. We've got to keep ahead of them, Hallie."

In her mind's eye, Hallie saw the entire village, armed and carrying torches, combing the woods for them. Could she and Adam and Becky outrun them? Even if they made it to the mountain path, what then? Could they manage to evade the villagers long enough to make it to the next town?

Yes. They had to. The people of Holyoake would never let them tell the world about all the sick things that went on in their evil, corrupt little village. Those people were playing for keeps.

But what if they do catch us? Hallie asked herself.

Then they mustn't discover Simon's part in this. As long as he's still free, maybe he can do something.

They had to drag Becky from her spot next to the stream, promising her that the stream grew prettier and more bubbly farther on, in order to get her moving again.

They moved along the muddy, slippery bank as rapidly as they dared, keeping clear of the trees and aided by the moonlight. Hallie lost her footing once, and plunged down the short incline into the stream. It was only a matter of a lost minute or two, but it left her wet and shaken.

Every now and then they'd stop and listen for pursuing villagers. They could hear trampling and shouting behind them in the woods, but from the sound of things, they had a good head start, and they kept up the pace in order to widen the gap between them and their pursuers.

The stream wound and looped through the woods.

"I think we must be roughly parallel with the road now," Adam said at one point, when it seemed as if they'd been running forever.

"How close are we?" Hallie asked breathlessly. "What if they come straight through from the road and find us?"

"I don't think they expect us to be where we are, Hallie. They probably think we went deep into the woods at the point where we ran off the road. We wouldn't have known about the stream if Simon hadn't told us, right? They must figure we don't know where we are and that we're back there fumbling around in the dark."

"Then maybe we have a better chance than we thought," Hallie said. "How much farther do you think it is to the mountain trail?"

"I don't know. It's hard to judge distance the way the stream loops and bends. Can you keep moving this fast? What about Becky? Does she seem okay to you?"

"She isn't saying anything, but she doesn't act tired." Hallie regretted having to talk about

Becky as if she weren't there. But she wasn't—not mentally, anyway.

"I haven't heard the villagers for a long time, have you? No shouting." Adam sounded out of breath. Hallie knew they were all running on pure adrenaline.

"No," Hallie told him. "I haven't heard anything either." She would have added that the silence bothered her. That it was almost too good to be true. But she needed to save her breath. Besides, why worry him?

"If someone's following us, we'd have seen them or heard them by now," Adam said. "They're a noisy bunch, and they'd have closed in on us long ago. We're going to make it, Hallie. Once we get on that mountain trail, we can keep to the underbrush. We ought to get to that little town Simon told us about before dawn."

Hallie tried to see her watch in the moonlight but couldn't. She figured that dawn couldn't be more than three hours away. In three hours they'd be safe. The nightmare would be over.

Just three more hours. When the sun comes up, we'll be drinking coffee in some nice little police station in a nice little all-American town. And then we'll come back to Holyoake with every police officer in the state and rescue Simon.

"There's the road we have to cross up ahead," Adam said, drawing Hallie and Becky back into the shelter of a clump of trees. "There, where the stream goes through the culvert, see?"

The road looked deserted, but they waited, watching, to make sure it was safe. Once they left the cover of the trees, they would be in plain sight until they reached the woods on the opposite side of the road.

"Wait until that cloud passes in front of the moon," Adam whispered. "Then we'll run across."

The cloud was shaped like an old Spanish galleon, and it sailed boldly across the face of the moon, blotting out the light. The road was plunged into darkness, and Adam and Hallie held tight to Becky's hands as they ran swiftly and silently over the uneven surface of the old country road.

And then the night was pierced with javelins of light, as what looked like half the people of Holyoake stepped out of the woods and surrounded Adam, Hallie, and Becky.

EIGHTEEN

"You were right, Vicar," said a triumphant voice. "They did just what you said they would."

More lights were emerging from the woods. More people encircling the three teens. Hallie, in a state of shock, found herself staring at them dazedly, unblinkingly, wondering where they had all come from.

The vicar stepped forward. In the dancing beams of the many flashlights, his pale face and white hair made him look spectral, like a creature from another time and place.

"There's no escape, you know. No running away," he told Hallie and Adam. "Surely you didn't think you could evade your fate. The fate that The Goddess has, in her infinite wisdom, arranged for you."

Adam glanced around frantically, as if looking for a way out, a hole in the crowd through which they could bolt, but the encircling villagers only pressed closer, shoulder to shoulder, cutting off any chance of escape. They all smiled diabolically, gloating over their victims.

Hallie knew how a rabbit must feel when surrounded by a pack of hungry wolves. These people were all but licking their lips!

"How'd you get here?" Adam demanded. "We thought you were behind us in the woods."

"We've been right here, waiting for you," the vicar replied smugly. "A few of our people have been following you quietly, but the rest of us were here, preparing a warm welcome for you."

He smiled unpleasantly. Even from where she stood, three or four feet away from him, Hallie could smell his stale, sour breath. Was everything in this town rotten and unclean?

"It was easier this way, you see," the vicar explained. "Oh, we *could* have chased you through the woods, adding to the drama of your pathetic escape attempt, but that would have been predictable. Vulgar. Offensive to The Goddess. When we found your footprints by the creek, we knew

immediately that you would try to follow it upstream in a foolish attempt to get over the mountains. And that you would have to cross the road
at this point."

Then he added with a sneer, "So we let you
think you'd lost us, and you fell right into our
trap. How stupid you were to think you could
outrun us when we've lived here for nearly three
hundred years! We know every inch of this
land."

Yes, we were stupid, Hallie thought. *Stupid
to believe we were actually escaping this evil
place. We've been doomed, right from the start.
And now Becky will be their Fire Maiden for
sure.*

She glanced quickly around the crowd. Simon
wasn't there. Nor was Mrs. Grigsby. Where were
they? Had Mrs. Grigsby suspected her nephew's
part in all this? Was she at home, guarding him?
Was Simon as doomed as they were?

The vicar turned his head and made a slight
signal to Elder Sidlaw, who was standing beside
him. The elder nodded, glanced over at Becky
and, in turn, signaled almost imperceptibly to
Brother William.

The two men moved forward silently until
they were standing, one on either side of Becky.

Then they each took an elbow and began to steer her through the crowd, which parted respectfully before them.

Becky, who had been silent up to now, suddenly became vocal.

"I don't want to go with you!" she protested, stopping dead in her tracks. "Let go of my arms. I want to stay with my friends."

"Where are you taking her?" Adam demanded, trying to push his way through the resisting crowd. "Let her go!"

"Now, Adam," the vicar said soothingly. "Surely you don't think we'd allow our lovely little Fire Maiden to remain with you. She must be prepared for tomorrow's ceremony."

"Ceremony? I know what you're planning to do with her!" Adam shouted. "And if you think you can commit a crime like that—"

"But it isn't a crime," the vicar responded piously. "It's a holy sacrifice. The will of The Goddess."

Again Adam tried to break through the crowd, to reach Becky, but two men grabbed him from behind, pinioning his arms. His frantic struggles to free himself only made them tighten their hold on him, bending him back in a painful arch. Then someone came forward with several lengths of rope, and the two men quickly tied Adam's legs together, then his arms.

"Becky!" Adam called helplessly.

One of the men threw a beefy arm around Adam's neck. Adam coughed and choked, unable to speak.

"Please don't take Becky!" Hallie begged the vicar. "Please!"

Becky stretched out an arm to her friends. "I want to go with them," she told her captors.

The vicar ignored Hallie and Adam and spoke directly to Becky. His tone of voice was that of someone speaking to a very young and not-too-bright child.

"Now, now, my dear, we're only taking you back to Mrs. Grigsby. You remember Mrs. Grigsby, don't you?" He accented the name both times, pausing to note Becky's reaction.

"Mrs. Grigsby?" Becky asked, dropping her arm. A dull, placid look came over her face. "Mrs. Grigsby?" she asked again.

"Yes, Mrs. Grigsby. She's waiting for you, and she's quite worried about you," the vicar said. "And she's very, very hurt, because you ran away without even saying good-bye. She's waiting at the Place of Worship."

"No!" Hallie shouted, throwing herself at the

vicar and trying to hit him with her clenched fists. "No! Not that terrible place! I saw the font with the bloodstains!"

Reverend Thoreson managed to push her away and signaled angrily to Norman, who rushed forward, grabbed her arms, and yanked her backward.

"Shall I tie her up, too?" Norman asked the vicar. He seemed eager for the job.

Slimy little scumbag, Hallie thought, kicking him in the ankle.

Norman grunted and twisted her arm viciously. "She's a wild one," he said. "I could hog-tie her."

The vicar shook his head regretfully. "No. No ropes on that one. The Goddess does not like us to bruise those whom we plan to destroy for Her sake. We already have one who is slightly damaged." He indicated Adam, who was struggling against his bonds. "So just hold the girl tight for now."

The headlights of a car lit up the road.

"Ah, here's your transportation back to the village," Reverend Thoreson told Becky. "And you'll like the driver. It's Sister Evans. You'll find her quite inspiring."

Becky only stared at him blankly, uncomprehendingly.

The car, an elderly Chevrolet sedan, pulled to a stop on the shoulder of the road. Sister Evans leaned across the passenger's seat and threw open the door. The interior light flashed on. She was a thin, bitter-faced woman with an unpleasant smile.

"Ah, Sister Evans," said Reverend Thoreson. "And not a moment too soon."

He waved Becky toward the car. Elder Sidlaw and Brother William escorted her through the crowd and gently helped her into the back seat. Then Brother William entered the car on Becky's left side, while Elder Sidlaw crawled in on the right. Becky was flanked on both sides. It would have been impossible for her to escape now, even if she'd been in any state to try. She sank back in the seat, looking straight ahead.

"What have you done to her?" Hallie sobbed. "What have you turned her into? What kind of people are you, anyway?"

Reverend Thoreson waved Sister Evans off with an elegant flutter of his hand.

The car sputtered briefly and started off down the road. Slowly, sedately, as befitted the bearer of the next Fire Maiden.

"Please don't leave Becky in that church," Hallie said again, shivering. "I know that you . . . you *kill* things in that church."

The vicar laughed mockingly. "In the first place we don't call it a church. It's our Place of Worship. There's a difference, you see. And yes, we do kill things there, but they are only minor sacrifices. Fowl. Small woodland creatures. Things of that nature."

"Then why do you need Becky? Let us go, and we won't tell a soul what goes on here. I promise!"

Norman snickered in Hallie's ear at that. He obviously found what she said amusing. The others must have, too, as a little ripple of laughter passed over the crowd.

"But our small sacrifices aren't satisfying The Goddess," Reverend Thoreson said in a calm, reasonable tone. "Our harvests have been poor. Our women are not producing healthy offspring. The Goddess has made it clear she needs a human sacrifice for Beltane."

"Your harvests are probably poor because you're farming the way people did three hundred years ago!" Hallie found she was shouting, so she lowered her voice, trying to sound reasonable. "Maybe the soil's worn out. And maybe your women would produce healthy children if you had a doctor in town, instead of Mrs. Grigsby and her herbs!"

"Yes, I'm sure you feel that way," the vicar replied. "You Outsiders think you know everything, don't you? But we here in Holyoake know the truth."

He turned to the villagers and asked, "Do you remember the last time? Our harvests? The sickly infants?"

"Yes, yes," they murmured, almost as if they were chanting in unison.

"But Sister Evans gave her only child, Deborah, to The Goddess and saved us all," called a woman in the rear of the crowd.

"Sister Evans? The woman in the car just now? You mean she actually let you kill her own daughter?" cried Hallie. "I can't believe it!"

That poor, poor girl! How could anyone do that to their own flesh and blood? How could anyone do that to anyone?

"Yes, Deborah Evans," Reverend Thoreson said dreamily. "And The Goddess smiled on us once again. The harvests were plentiful. Healthy children were born."

"You're crazy, all of you. Can't you see? It was just a coincidence! Please don't kill us. Our dying won't change a thing!"

Hallie was shouting now, but she didn't care. She *had* to convince them. Surely they could see what a terrible mistake they were making!

The vicar seemed to snap out of his reverie. "But why are we wasting time when there are so many things to do?"

He beckoned to several of his followers. "Brother Norman's truck is parked beyond that next bend. Please help escort our guests to it. We wouldn't want them to make another pointless attempt at escape, would we?"

The burly man removed his arm from Adam's throat and threw Adam bodily over his shoulder as if he were carrying a sack of grain.

Adam managed to raise his head and look at Hallie.

"It's no use, Hallie," he croaked. "These people are all insane."

Norman pushed Hallie along before him, still holding her arms twisted cruelly behind her. "So you did have a car all along, Norman," she said. "I figured you were lying."

Norman sneered. "You Outsiders are supposed to be so smart about modern things. You kids could have fixed your own car. There really wasn't that much wrong with it . . . before I got my hands on it."

The bumpy ride in the back of Norman's old wooden-sided truck seemed to last an eternity. It was dark—still no sign of dawn. Hallie remembered how she'd thought that dawn would see her safe in a police station somewhere and felt her stomach turn over with fear.

What would dawn bring now?

And would she have the courage to face it?

NINETEEN

Hallie was grimly surprised to see that she and Adam were being returned to Mrs. Grigsby's house. The neat, white house on the edge of the Green seemed too normal a place in which to await execution.

Yes, execution. There was no other word for it. She and Adam had to deal with the fact that they would be killed immediately after Becky's public burning.

"Just a little something extra for The Goddess" was the way Reverend Thoreson had put it when they parted. He made it sound so reasonable. So harmless. Hallie and Adam—a couple of last-minute Beltane add-ons to help make the corn harvest a smash success this year.

Norman and the others brought them into the house through the cellar entrance.

It must have been a part of the old, original house, Hallie noted, because the steps were crude and uneven and ended in what appeared to be some sort of storage area—a series of damp, musty rooms with bumpy dirt floors and low, beamed ceilings.

The room Hallie and Adam found themselves in was the one farthest away from the steps and the most strongly built and heavily reinforced room in the cellar. The door was of thick oak, studded with iron nails, and the room's one window was set high in the wall and was barred with heavy, wrought-iron crosspieces.

Escape would be impossible.

Is this some kind of prison? Hallie wondered. *How many people doomed for execution in the name of The Goddess spent their last nights here?*

Adam, still bound hand and foot, had been carried into the room and dumped on the floor like a sack of potatoes. He grunted when he landed, and he tried to sit up.

"You can untie him if you feel like it, Missy,"

his captor said, grinning. "It will give you some-thing to do . . . while you wait."

While we wait. For Becky's horrible death. And ours.

How would they die, Adam and she? At least not by fire. That was evidently being saved for the Fire Maiden. So how? What had the vicar said about The Goddess not wanting her offer-ings bruised or damaged? Did that mean they would be suffocated? Or drowned? Poisoned, maybe? Those were the only ways of being killed she could think of at the moment that didn't leave marks.

Maybe it won't be too painful. Maybe they'll do it quickly. Maybe they'll give us something to knock us out first. One of Mrs. Grigsby's herbs. Maybe we won't even see it coming.

Maybe.

Hallie bent over Adam. He wasn't saying any-thing. Just half-sitting, half-lying there. She knew those ropes must hurt. So why wasn't he saying anything?

"I'll have those ropes off you in a couple of minutes, Adam."

Still no answer.

Hallie broke a couple of fingernails untying the knots that held him. She almost smiled, remembering how she used to think that a broken fingernail or a zit before a big date was such a tragedy.

"That feels better, Hallie," Adam said, rubbing the circulation back into his ankles. "Thanks."

He didn't meet her eyes but just sat looking down at his feet.

"Look, Adam," she told him. "You put up a good fight back there, but we didn't have a chance. There was nothing we could have done to escape."

Now he looked up and met her gaze. "I don't feel that way. I feel responsible for getting us all into this mess—Becky, you, me. God, Hallie, I'm about to go crazy."

Hallie sat beside him and leaned back against the rough stone wall.

"None of this is your fault," she told him. "It just happened."

When he didn't reply, she went on. "You know, Adam, all our lives our parents and teachers have tried to keep us from hurting ourselves. How many times have they told us not to run with scissors in our hands? Not to go out in the snow bareheaded? But nobody ever told us not to visit a pretty little village where the people believe in human sacrifice, did they?"

Adam smiled faintly and Hallie felt encouraged. She didn't want Adam going to his death feeling as though he'd let Becky and her down. He'd always been a good friend and one of the nicest people Hallie knew. Above all, she didn't want him to die thinking it was all his fault.

"That damn van, though," he mumbled. "I never should have bought it. If I hadn't, we wouldn't be here now."

"Lots of kids our age buy cars that turn out to be lemons. That doesn't mean they're going to wind up in a place like Holyoake," she said.

Adam patted her on the shoulder. "You're okay, you know that, Hallie?"

If only I felt as brave as I sound, Hallie thought.

"Look, Hallie," Adam said, beginning to sound like himself again. "It's not over yet. The Beltane ceremony is still hours away. Maybe we can get out of this place."

He stood up and shook his legs, first one, then the other. "My feet are still asleep."

Hallie got up too. "You're right. We can't just give up. Then we really *will* go crazy. At least we can go down fighting." Hallie looked around the room. "The door is thick, though, and there's a huge bolt on the outside—I noticed it when we came in. No chance of getting out that way."

"If the bolt's on the outside, they must keep things locked up in here, right?" Adam asked grimly. "Probably things that try to escape."

"That's what I've been thinking," Hallie said. "This place must double as a jail. And I guess that means we aren't the first people to be put in here for safekeeping. The men who brought us seemed to take it for granted we can't get away."

"I wonder if this is where they kept Simon's folks. Before they . . . you know," said Adam.

"I've been afraid even to think of him for fear of jinxing him," Hallie said. "He wasn't in the woods with the others, Adam. I'm scared they know he was the one who told us about following the stream up over the mountains."

"But they didn't say anything about him," Adam reminded her. "Maybe he's over at the church with Mrs. Grigsby."

"I hope so. I'd hate to think we got him into danger, too."

"Well, there's nothing we can do about Simon now," Adam said. "Our only chance of helping him is to get out of here ourselves, if we can."

But the odds are we can't, Hallie thought. *After all, Simon's parents lived here. If they didn't know how to break out of this cellar, there's no way we'll know how.*

"We could try the window," Adam suggested hopefully. "Those bars look old and rusty. Maybe we can work them loose."

The moonlight streamed in through the barred window, making a pattern of crosses on the wall. Hallie looked up at the beamed ceiling. "I guess this room wouldn't have any kind of light fixture, would it?"

"I can't see one," Adam answered. "This place probably started out as an old-fashioned root cellar. They never bothered to put in electricity."

On the far wall were several rows of shelves. Hallie went over to them. "Maybe I can find a lantern or a candle."

She groped around and finally found the stub of a candle. Holding it up to the moonlight, she could see that it was ragged, chewed. She remembered hearing how mice and rats loved wax and nearly threw the candle to the ground in revulsion. Ugh! To be touching something some filthy rodent had been chewing on!

But this was a new Hallie. Instead, she felt around among—probably—rat droppings, searching for matches. There were none.

"I've got a candle but no matches," she

reported. "You don't have any, do you?"

"Are you kidding? You know I don't smoke. It shortens your life expectancy," he said glumly.

"I guess we'll have to work by moonlight, then," Hallie said.

Adam was standing at the window on a large wooden box he'd found, reaching up and yanking on the bars. "These bars are so old, they give a little when I pull on them."

Hallie tried not to get her hopes up. "Do you think there's a chance we can pry them loose?"

"Maybe not pry, but we can try to pull them out."

Adam unbuckled his belt and removed it. Then he attached it to one of the bars, pulling the belt through the buckle. He gave it a couple of tugs, testing it.

"Come on, Hallie," he said, helping her up on the box. "Maybe if we both pull . . ."

They pulled and pulled in unison. The bars wobbled a little but didn't give.

"They're embedded too deep in the stone window frame," Adam said at last. "I'll have to try to dig them out."

"Do you have a pocketknife?" Hallie asked. "You know, one of those Swiss Army things?"

Adam looked at her with an odd expression on his face. "My mother never let us have pocketknives. She was afraid we'd hurt ourselves."

It was too much. Hallie and Adam both burst into wild, hysterical laughter.

After a moment Hallie caught her breath. She felt better. "Maybe we can find something to use as a shovel—an old spoon. A tin can. Anything."

Adam looked down at his belt buckle. It was large, heavy, and made of some kind of metal.

"My cousin sent me this from Texas," he said. "It's a genuine Dallas Cowboys belt buckle. And it's got this big hook on the back. See? Where it's supposed to fit into the holes in the belt. Maybe I can dig the bars out with it."

He attacked the masonry around the iron bars.

Hallie watched as he gouged valiantly at the stone. Hours seemed to go by. Actually it was only minutes, from what she could see by a moonlight check of her watch. Finally Adam uttered a muffled curse.

"What happened?" Hallie asked.

"The hook broke off," Adam replied testily. "I've always been a Redskins fan myself."

"Did you loosen the bars any?"

"No. That stone looks old and wobbly, but it's pretty strong. I'm afraid it would take a masonry drill to dig those bars out of there."

Neither spoke for a moment. Finally Hallie said, "Listen! Did you hear that?"

"What?"

"Birds. I heard chirping. That means dawn is about to break."

Dawn. May the first. Beltane.

The bonfire. The bonefire. The sacrifice of the Fire Maiden.

And where was Becky right now? Was Mrs. Grigsby keeping her doped up with those herbs of hers?

Hallie fervently wished that Becky would be so heavily drugged she would be spared the suffering of the flames. Becky, the Fire Maiden, the human sacrifice that would supposedly bring fertility and the blessings of the mythical Goddess to this loathsome place.

"Dawn?" Adam said. "But it's still pitch black out there."

"Haven't you ever heard that it's always darkest before dawn?" Hallie asked him. "In just a little while the sun will rise, and . . ." Her voice trailed away.

"And Becky will die. Then us," Adam said. He sat down heavily and put his hands over his face.

There was a movement at the window. A face thrust through the iron bars.

"Simon!" Hallie yelped.

"I'm sorry I couldn't get here sooner," he whispered. "When the signal guns went off, Aunt Phoebe made me stay with her. And then the vicar summoned me after you'd been brought back to Holyoake. He's had me with him and the elders all this time, talking about tomorrow."

He pressed closer against the bars.

"Listen to me," he commanded. "Don't give up. I've got a plan."

TWENTY

Hallie hopped up on the box. She was so glad to see him, she could have kissed him, even through the bars.

"Simon!" she said again. "We've been so worried about you. We thought maybe they knew you'd helped us and—"

"Some help," he said. "You didn't get very far."

"That didn't have anything to do with you," Hallie said. "Becky was so out of it she decided to chat with the guards."

Adam joined them at the window. "Better keep it down," he cautioned. "Someone might hear you."

Simon looked back anxiously over his shoulder.

"Right. We don't have much time—we've got a lot to talk about if we're going to get you out of here."

"We're getting out of here?" Hallie echoed. "Please don't tell us that if it's not true. It only makes things worse."

Against her will, tears puddled up in her eyes and ran silently down her cheeks.

"I wouldn't do that, Hallie." Simon reached through the bars and took her hand. His face was level with hers.

What a kind face he has, Hallie thought. *Why didn't I notice that right from the start?*

"I really mean it," Simon was saying. "There *is* a way out of here."

"How?" Adam asked in a low, tense voice. "Will it put you in any danger?"

"No," Simon said. "They don't suspect me in the least. I've managed to convince them that helping out with the Beltane sacrifice is my top priority."

He's supposed to kill me, Hallie remembered. *That's how he's supposed to help out with Beltane.*

"Here's the situation," Simon told them. "There's only one person guarding you, and he's up in the kitchen. Aunt Phoebe's over in the

Place of Worship with Becky and—"

"What are they doing to Becky?" Adam broke in worriedly. "They aren't hurting her, are they?"

"No. She's okay. They've got her so doped up, she doesn't know who or where she is. They don't want her to figure out what's going on and put up a fight."

"Good," Hallie said. What had been worrying her most was the thought that Becky would become aware of what the villagers were planning to do to her. She was glad now that Mrs. Grigsby was keeping her zonked out.

"Can you handle the guard in the kitchen?" Adam asked.

"No problem. I'll knock him out with one of my aunt's teas. I know more about her herbs than she realizes. Once he's unconscious, I'll come down here and unbolt your door."

"When are you going to do all this? Right away?" Adam asked.

"No. It will have to be just before the start of Beltane. Right now Reverend Thoreson and all the elders are over in the Place of Worship with Becky. They'll be there until about an hour before the festival."

"Why are they all with Becky?" Hallie asked uneasily.

"It's kind of an all-night pray-in to The Goddess, to soften her up for the big one tomorrow."

And they're probably killing a couple of chickens for good measure, Hallie thought with a shudder, remembering the bloodstained marble font.

"Okay, so you drug the guard and then what?" Adam asked. "We can't go out on the street. Someone's sure to recognize us."

"Not if you wear a costume," replied Simon. "Everyone wears medieval costumes with masks for the festival. I can get my hands on a couple of masks, but finding the costumes is going to take some doing."

Hallie and Adam exchanged excited glances.

"We brought our costumes for the Shakespeare Festival with us," Hallie said. "They'll be perfect. With masks on, we'll fit right in."

"I can't believe this!" Simon said. "It's almost too good to be true."

"Wait a minute," Adam put in. "Maybe it is too good to be true. Won't our costumes stick out like sore thumbs? I mean, isn't everybody used to seeing everybody else in the same old getups, year after year?"

"No, as a matter of fact, we aren't," Simon

told him. "People make their own costumes. Everyone wears a different one each year. That's the big thing around here. People keep their costumes secret, so their neighbors will have to guess who's who."

"Okay," Hallie said, glancing up at the sky, which was growing lighter every minute. "So what happens next? The guard's out cold in the kitchen, and Adam and I run upstairs and put on our costumes. Then what? How are we going to get out of town?"

"And what about Becky?" Adam asked. "I'm not leaving here without her."

"Me neither," Hallie agreed. "It's got to be all three of us or none."

"That's the hard part," Simon said, "and we're going to have to improvise a little as we go. But for starters, we'll need a getaway car."

"Whose?" Adam asked. "There aren't many cars of any kind in this town. And I bet even your Aunt Phoebe could outrun Brother William's Model T."

"I was thinking of Norman's truck," Simon said. "Most of the cars are kept under lock and key in Holyoake. Reverend Thoreson holds the keys. You have to go to him for permission to leave town."

"I guess that keeps runaway attempts to a minimum," Adam put in.

"That's the general idea," Simon agreed. "The only person who's allowed to keep his own key is Norman, since he owns the only truck in the village and needs to use it all the time."

"Won't it be locked up, too, because of the festival?" Hallie asked.

"No. It will be outside. Parked on the Green. Maybe even in front of the Place of Worship. You see—" he paused for a moment, as if unsure whether or not he should continue "—you see, after the burning, they plan to load all the ashes from the bonfire into the truck. Then they'll take them out and scatter them over the fields at the edge of town. To fertilize the crops. It's a part of the ceremony."

"And Becky's ashes are supposed to be mixed in with them. She's supposed to make the fields more fertile," Hallie whispered. "That's what you're saying, isn't it?

Simon nodded.

"Well, it's not going to happen," Adam vowed. "She'll ride in that truck all right. But she'll be alive when she does it."

"Right!" said Hallie. "But what about the key to the truck? How do we get hold of it?"

"It will be in the ignition," Simon said. "Norman always does that."

"So we have Norm's truck parked on the Green with the keys in the ignition. But how will we kidnap Becky?" Adam said.

"She'll be in the Place of Worship with Aunt Phoebe. They'll know she's drugged, and they'll think you two are safely locked up, so they won't feel it's necessary to have any guards watching her," Simon said. "The three of us can sneak in, overpower Aunt Phoebe, and drive off with Becky."

"What if they follow us?" Hallie said.

"They'll have to get the keys to their cars first, and then get them out of the barns where they're kept locked up. We'll be miles away before they're even ready to start out after us."

"How fast does Norm's truck go?" Adam asked. "It was moving pretty slowly when he brought us here. Don't we need something speedy if we're going to make a quick getaway?"

"Norman likes to tinker with engines—you know that," Simon told him. "When he wants to, he can make that thing go pretty fast, not that the vicar ever lets him."

Hallie looked at him doubtfully.

"Look, Hallie," Simon said. "It's going to be

okay. We're going to get out of this town alive. All of us."

"Does that mean you're coming, too?"

"Yes. The guard will know what I did to him when he recovers from his tea. But in the meantime I'll tie him up and drag him down here, so there's no chance he can come to and spoil things for us."

"What time does the festival start?" Adam asked.

"Around ten o'clock. Everyone will be out on the Green at least an hour before that, though, and Aunt Phoebe will be alone with Becky, so that's when we should make our move."

The sky behind Simon was beginning to show streaks of pink.

"I've got to go," he said hurriedly. "Here." He shoved a flashlight through the bars of the window. "Take this. You might need it."

Then he smiled at Hallie and said, "Come closer to the window."

She did, pressing her face against the bars. And then, to her surprise, he kissed her through the grids.

"For luck," he said.

Hallie smiled up at him. "We're going to make it, Simon."

"Absolutely," Simon said, and disappeared as suddenly as he'd come.

Adam was prowling the cellar, shining the flashlight into all the dark corners. Suddenly he stopped, his light on a section of the wall by the door.

"What is it?" Hallie asked. "What are you looking at?"

"Nothing," he said, quickly switching off the light.

She went over to him. "Show me what you saw, Adam. You're only making me imagine the worst."

He trained the light on the wall. "No wonder Simon's parents decided to run away. The village must have locked up the Fire Maidens—or at least the unwilling ones—down here. Maybe Aunt Phoebe hadn't gotten clever with her herbs yet."

His hand suddenly began to tremble, and Hallie had to hold it steady in order to see what was on the wall.

A name—and something else—was scratched unevenly into one of the flat stones:

DEBORAH EVANS
MAY 1, 1985
FORGET ME NOT

TWENTY-ONE

It was nearly ten o'clock when Hallie and Adam heard Simon slide back the bolt and open the cellar door.

They'd been pacing the cell for what seemed hours, their nerves on edge, listening to the voices of the people gathering on the Green. Wondering with growing fear what had happened to Simon. Worrying that their plans had been discovered and that he'd been taken prisoner.

Simon's face was white and tense. He breathlessly explained the reasons for his delay as he hustled Hallie and Adam up the inner stairway that led to the kitchen.

"Aunt Phoebe came home. I didn't expect her,

but she said she'd left her Beltane costume here and that Becky was out cold so . . . It took her forever to change. . . . She finally left, and then I had trouble getting Jem Woodley, the guard, to drink his tea. . . . He kept saying he wanted coffee instead. I nearly had to hit him over the head to get the tea into him."

He pushed open the heavy, creaking door that led into the kitchen. A large, inert body lay on the floor, bound hand and foot.

"You're going to have to help me drag him downstairs, Adam," Simon said. "He weighs a ton."

"I'll go change into my costume," Hallie said. "And I'll lay yours out on your bed, Adam. We don't have much time."

She could hear them thumping down the cellar stairs, carrying Jem between them, as she ran up to her room.

With shaking hands, she rummaged in the closet for her costume, yanking it off its hanger. Then she stripped off her jeans and sweater and pulled the dress over her head, thankful as she did that the dressmaker had sewn a long polyester zipper down the back instead of little hooks or buttons. Kicking off her sneakers, she slipped into the flimsy, black kid slippers that went with the dress. It would be a problem to have to run in these things, she knew, but the sneakers would be a dead giveaway if anyone looked at her feet.

A quick glance in the mirror told her she looked great, in spite of her hurried dressing. But her hair! That long black hair hanging down her back would make her stick out like a sore thumb in this pale-haired community.

She couldn't find her comb, so she raked her hair back from her face with her fingers, twisted it into a thick rope and coiled it high on her head, securing it with a handful of hairpins. Then, after a quick search in the bureau drawer, she found a large, plain-colored scarf, which she tied around her head peasant style, making sure her hair was completely covered.

She was in Adam's room, laying his costume on the bed, when she heard him on the stairs—taking them two at a time by the sound of it. She'd just found the shoes for his costume when he burst into the room.

"The festival's going to be starting soon," he panted. "I'll never get into those pantyhose things in time."

"Tights are easier to get into than your diving wet suit," she told him as he flung off his sweatshirt and pulled on his shirt and tunic. "Just put

197

them on one leg at a time and make sure both toes are pointing forward."

He was grunting and cursing as she ran downstairs to the kitchen where Simon waited, shifting impatiently from one foot to the other.

Simon, she noticed, looked pretty cute in *his* tights.

Their masks were laid out on the table. Hallie was relieved to see that they covered the face completely. That would help conceal their identities. She tied hers on and, in a muffled voice, asked, "How do I look?"

"Medieval. It's hard to believe a beautiful girl is under all that."

Beautiful? Under her all-concealing mask, Hallie felt a warm blush travel up her face.

Now was definitely not the time to think about things like that.

Adam thundered down the stairs and into the kitchen. His face was red. His hair ruffled. His hose were sagging and twisted around his legs and snagged in several places where, it appeared, his fingernails had gone right through them.

Wordlessly Simon clapped a mask on Adam's face and tied it behind him before putting on his own.

"Are we ready?" he asked, pulling his hood

over his head and gesturing for Adam to do the same.

Hallie drew a trembling breath. "Ready."

They had to slip out the back door and come onto the Green separately so no one would recognize them. It was hard not to break into a run. The Beltane festival was slated to start soon, and they had so much to do before that.

A crowd had gathered on the Green. There was a sort of frenzied merriment in the air. Laughs were too loud. People were too animated.

Hallie, Adam, and Simon met, outwardly casual, inwardly churning with nerves, in front of the Place of Worship.

"Where's Norman's truck?" Hallie hissed from beneath her mask. "I've looked all over and it's not here!"

"Maybe he's late," Adam suggested hopefully. "Maybe the ceremony's been delayed."

"I'll ask around," Simon told them. "Someone here must know where he is. In the meantime, you guys walk around. Look like everybody else." He loped off across the Green.

Hallie squeezed Adam's arm as they walked. "It's going to work, Adam. We just have to keep our cool. But once we're out of this place, I'm going to have the granddaddy of all nervous breakdowns!"

"I don't know, Hallie. I have this strange feeling something's going to go wrong."

Hallie didn't answer. Maybe Adam was right. There were so many things that *could* go wrong. Starting with Norman's truck.

Where *was* Norman's truck?

And if he didn't show up, how were they going to escape with Becky?

Hallie saw Reverend Thoreson and the elders meeting in the center of the Green. They were in costume for the ceremony. The elders all wore scarlet robes and hoods.

Red for burning! Hallie thought with a sick feeling.

The reverend was in a trailing white robe with long, wide sleeves, and he wore a wreath of leaves on his head. It was plain to see he was the leader of this disgusting festival.

And in just a little while he and the elders would enter the church and escort Becky to the flames. . . .

Hallie looked around. The villagers were milling about the Green. A couple of booths, draped in garlands and spring flowers, had been set up, and people were selling what looked like little pies and cakes. Several games of chance were going on at tables set up on the other end of the Green, accompanied by wild shouts of laughter.

The feeling of expectation and excitement ran like an electric current through the crowd. Hallie wondered if it had been like this the last time, ten years ago, when they'd burned poor Deborah Evans.

Forget me not, Deborah had carved into the wall of her cell. *Forget me not.* Like something from a sixth-grade autograph book. She must have known she'd be memorialized as a Fire Maiden. But obviously Deborah, frightened and alone, had wanted to be remembered for herself— a young girl forced to die before her time.

A number of couples had taken their places at the Maypole, streamers in their right hands. The fiddler nodded at them and began to play. They danced, sedately at first, weaving in and out, neatly braiding the streamers that hung from the top of the pole. Then the fiddler's music grew bolder and wilder, and the dancers moved faster and faster in response.

Hallie had gone to a rock concert once where the loudness of the music and the gyrations of the musicians had caused a kind of mob hysteria, and the police had had to rush in and restore order.

The Maypole dance reminded her of that. It wasn't anywhere as loud or as raucous as the rock concert. As a matter of fact, it was almost sedate in comparison. But there was something about it, something she couldn't put her finger on, that was even more threatening, more sensual, than that concert.

Hallie was frightened. Something evil was loose in the air. She could sense it.

Oh, where is Simon?

"Look over at the oak tree," Adam said. "What are those people doing?"

The ancient oak was heavily festooned with floral garlands, its withered branches drooping under their weight. Some young women were clinging to the tree and embracing it, kissing it, taking wreaths from their hair and adding them to the garlands already there. Others, watching them, clapped and cheered, joining hands and dancing around the tree.

"They're all nuts," Adam said. "Every last one of them. Do you think they're tanked up on one of Mrs. Grigsby's brews?"

Simon came toward them over the grass, not obviously hurrying, but rapidly closing the distance between them.

"We're in trouble," he said in a low voice. "Norman's not here."

"Where is he?" Adam asked. "Where's his truck?"

"Someone just told me he's gone off to the fields, to get things ready for later, when they scatter the ashes."

"But he's supposed to be here now!" Hallie hissed through clenched teeth. "You said he's supposed to be here now!"

"I know." Simon's words came out ragged, breathless. "But he's going to wait, they said, until just after the ceremony."

"We've got to have wheels if we're going to rescue Becky," Adam said frantically.

Suddenly the sky darkened as a cloud drifted in front of the sun.

It had been threatening rain all morning, with black clouds on the horizon and the occasional rumble of far-off thunder.

"Maybe it will rain," Hallie said. "Maybe they'll cancel the bonfire."

"No," Simon said. "Look over there. I think they're planning to speed up the ceremony."

Two men, dressed in multicolored tights and tunics, appeared on the edge of the Green, just in front of the church. They were carrying long-stemmed trumpets of some sort. The men raised the trumpets to their lips in unison and blew several ear-shattering blasts.

The crowd looked over toward the trumpeters and began to chatter excitedly. This was what they'd come for.

"Oh, God, Hallie," Adam said in her ear. "It's starting. We'll need a tank to get Becky out of here now!"

Hallie spun around and stared at him through the eyeholes in her mask. "A *tank*?"

She pulled Simon closer to her and Adam.

"Listen, you two," she whispered excitedly. "I've got a plan!"

TWENTY-TWO

The tricky part, she told them, would be the timing. A couple of minutes too soon or too late and they'd fail in their attempt to save Becky.

"We'll have to wait until they bring Becky out," she'd told them in a voice that was barely audible amid the surrounding hubbub. "We can't leave the Green until then, when all eyes are on her, or we'll be noticed."

Simon squeezed her arm. "You're wonderful, Hallie."

Adam was looking over their heads to the spot on the Green where Reverend Thoreson and the elders had been. "They're going into the church now." His voice was calm.

Hallie, pressed up close to him as she was, could see that his eyes had narrowed and that he'd squared his shoulders and clenched his fists. She'd seen Adam in basketball games many times, and this is how he always looked when the score was close and he was determined to win.

She knew how he felt because, surprisingly, she was no longer frightened or nervous. She was furious. At every single person in Holyoake for what they wanted to do to Becky—gentle, loving Becky, her dearest and oldest friend.

The trumpets blasted again. As if in echo, another roll of thunder sounded out in the surrounding countryside. The thunder was growing closer—but not close enough, Hallie knew, to help them now.

A third fanfare, and the doors of the church were flung open.

The chattering ceased, and all eyes were trained on the emerging procession.

First came the elders in their scarlet robes, carrying flaming torches. Under their hoods, their faces looked smug and odiously self-righteous.

Then came Reverend Thoreson with Becky, who was walking slowly and with difficulty. Her head drooped, and the vicar seemed to be holding her upright. She was obviously heavily sedated, because she stumbled and nearly fell several times. She was dressed in a long white gown and crowned with flower wreaths. The wreaths were hanging lopsidedly over one eye.

Mrs. Grigsby followed close behind, beaming.

Like the matron of honor at a wedding, Hallie noted with loathing. The old lady was even wearing a white gown in honor of the occasion.

A little cheer went up at the appearance of the main event, followed by a flutter of applause.

As the elders, the vicar, and Becky proceeded toward the pyre, Simon nodded almost imperceptibly to Hallie and Adam, and one by one, they quietly slipped away from the crowd.

Hallie hugged the edge of the Green, stopping frequently to make sure she hadn't been detected, but she soon realized no one was watching her. Every eye was trained on Becky, the Fire Maiden. No one wanted to miss one cry. One expression of agony. They'd waited ten long years for a show like this, and they wanted to milk it for all it was worth.

They say they're doing this for The Goddess, Hallie thought disgustedly, *but it's really for them. They're evil and cruel, and this is how they get their kicks.*

She saw Adam and Simon waiting for her behind a house that bordered the alley that would take them, unseen, to Norman's general store. They beckoned frantically, and she slipped across the lawn, keeping as close as she could to the shelter of the boxwood hedges that grew in such profusion in Holyoake.

"Hurry!" commanded Adam as they ran down the alley.

One of Hallie's kid slippers fell off as she ran, but she didn't stop to retrieve it. She was out of breath and gasping from a stitch in her side by the time they raced around the side of Norman's store, past the garage, to the shed that held the village fire engine.

"Damn! The door's locked!" Adam said, yanking on a huge, ancient padlock. "You'd think they'd keep it open and ready for action."

"Stand back," Simon said, picking up a large rock and bashing the padlock once, twice, three times. The lock dropped open, and he tore it from the hasp and threw it to the ground.

The three of them flung open the wide double doors and ran inside.

The fire engine sat waiting in its newly painted, well-tended glory. Waiting, as it always did, with a full tank of gas and an even fuller tank of water. Waiting to perform its heroic job as village fire extinguisher.

Only, today it would be called on to extinguish the fires of Beltane.

Adam opened the door on the driver's side of the fire engine and peered inside. "Norm didn't leave the keys in the ignition. Are they on the wall somewhere?"

Hallie looked on both sides of the door. "I can't see them anywhere. What about you, Simon?"

"No. Do you suppose he keeps them under the floor mat?"

Adam lifted the mats and pawed around frantically. Then he lowered the sun visors. Nothing. "We're wasting time. I'll have to hot-wire it."

He reached under the dashboard by the ignition switch, did something with a couple of wires, and within seconds he had the engine going.

"Okay, Hallie. It's all yours," he said as he backed out.

"I've never driven a gearshift car before, you know, much less a fire engine," she said nervously, crawling behind the wheel.

"Now you tell me," he groaned.

"You can do it, Hallie," Simon said reassuringly. "You have to. Adam and I will be manning the water pumps."

"The gears are like the letter H," Adam instructed. "It's easy. The top left corner of the H is reverse. Bottom left is first gear. Top right, second gear. Bottom right, third. Got it?"

"Yeah," Hallie mumbled. "I think."

She noticed, to her relief, that a diagram of the gears had been drawn into the hard rubber knob of the gearshift.

"Are you ready?" she shouted to the boys, who had taken up their positions on the back of the truck.

"Ready!" they shouted back.

Out on the Green, Hallie knew, Becky was being led like a sheep to the slaughter by Reverend Thoreson. Up the steps to the platform and then to the stake.

In just a few seconds those evil, leering elders would be lighting the fires.

Hallie threw the truck into reverse and stomped on the gas pedal.

The truck, bucking and lurching, careened backward out of the shed, ripping off one of the shed's wooden doors. Hallie tromped on the brake, relieved to see, after a quick glance in the rearview mirror, that the boys were still hanging on. Sure, they were yelling something angry and unintelligible at her, but they were hanging on.

So far, so good, Hallie thought. She squinted down at the diagram on the gearshift knob, then rammed it into first gear, stepped on the gas, and yanked the wheel in the general direction of the Green.

The truck responded with an enthusiastic roar. When she thought it was moving fast enough, she shifted into second, then into third, the truck leaping and shuddering each time. At one point she felt she was riding a bucking bronco as it lurched and dropped, lurched and dropped, down the alley toward the Green.

Hallie disregarded the terrified shouts from the back of the truck.

There was the Green, dead ahead. Becky was being tied to the stake, and the elders were holding their flaming torches aloft, obviously eager to touch them to the dried timber and start the so-called ceremony.

Hallie roared across the road, up and over the curb, narrowly missing a lamppost, as she headed toward the Green. Reverend Thoreson was putting the finishing touches on Becky's bonds.

As if a part of the script, multiple flashes of lightning suddenly illumined the sky, followed by claps of thunder that came rolling, reverberating down the valley.

Almost in answer to the thunder, the ululating scream of the fire truck's siren filled the air, and the red light atop the truck began to rotate, shooting out scarlet flashes. Hallie, carried away by the spirit of the moment, had hit every button on the dash.

The crowd scattered, screaming, as the truck hurtled toward them down the long, well-manicured length of the village Green. The carefully choreographed ceremony dissolved into shambles.

Reverend Thoreson took in the situation with one quick glance. Realizing he must now act quickly if the sacrificial rite was to take place, he signaled the elders to throw their torches on the dried wood and bones of the bonfire.

The fire caught hold rapidly, and little curls of smoke began to rise heavenward.

As the wood and bones began to burn, Hallie, steering erratically, crashed into the center of the flickering pyre and came to a screeching halt just in front of the stake where Becky, still unaware, was tethered.

Then, fearful that the flames might blow up her gas tank, Hallie frantically threw the truck into reverse with a dreadful grinding of gears. The truck shot backward, knocking down a couple of red-robed elders.

The dried wood and bones caught fire surprisingly quickly.

Simon had started the water pump on the rear of the tanker as they'd left the shed, and now he and Adam grabbed the two hoses, jumped down from the truck and began spraying first the rapidly growing fire that surrounded Becky, then the people who were now surging toward them, shouting.

Simon, adjusting the nozzle, directed a steady stream of water at Reverend Thoreson, knocking him off his feet. In the meantime Adam dropped his hose, which writhed and twisted like a snake on the ground, and raced up the steps to free Becky.

Simon trained his hose on the crowd, keeping them back.

Up on the platform, Becky, still under the influence of Mrs. Grigsby's drugs, resisted slightly as Adam quickly untied Reverend Thoreson's ineffectual knots. Then Adam grabbed Becky under her arms and hauled her over the wet, smoking bones to the truck. Holding her under one arm, he managed to yank open the passenger's-side door and thrust her inside, slamming the door behind her.

In the meantime Simon continued to spray

the worshipers of Holyoake with a steady stream of high-pressure water.

"Okay! Let's go!" Adam shouted, picking up his hose and jumping back on the truck.

He and Simon clung desperately to the truck, still managing to direct a stream of water at their pursuers, as they sped across the Green.

Reverend Thoreson crawled to his feet and attempted to take off after them, but Simon trained the hose on him and scored a direct hit. The reverend went down for the second, and final, time.

The storm had moved in closer, and another bolt of lightning flashed over the church steeple, hitting the lightning rod. Hallie, through the rearview mirror, saw a sizzling blue flame trace the outline of the steeple and the church.

The thunder reverberated all around them now, as on the ground the wet, bedraggled villagers picked themselves up and began to scream helplessly.

The sound of their screaming was drowned out by a mighty clap of thunder that accompanied, almost simultaneously, the huge forked bolt of lightning that hit the holy oak, cleaving its trunk and striking with deadly force those who huddled for shelter beneath its outspread branches.

The dry wood of the ancient oak burst into flames immediately, each branch a torch.

Hard upon the heels of the lightning came a mighty wind, scattering the fire throughout the village.

Hallie struggled with the wheel as the truck headed into the wind the storm had brought. Behind her she could see the fire spreading from the holy oak to the wooden houses that faced the Green. They were going up like tinder. Shrill screams split the air.

"Too bad we've got the only fire truck in town," she heard Adam shout at Simon.

"Good-bye, Holyoake, and good riddance!" Simon shouted back.

The barricade on the road leading from town was still in place, but those supposedly manning it were running frantically past them, back toward the doomed, burning village.

Hallie didn't stop, even though there was no one pursuing them any longer. She stomped harder, exultantly, on the gas pedal and crashed through the barricade, sending it flying skyward.

She could hear the boys behind her cheering her on.

Her hand on the wheel was surer now, more skillful, as they raced forward toward safety. She was getting the hang of this gearshift driving at long last. It really wasn't as complicated as it seemed.

On the seat beside her, Becky stirred, then sat up. Her eyes were clear.

"Wh—where am I?" she asked.

Hallie, eyes on the road, grinned happily. "I'd say you've just come home."

Becky looked over at Hallie and gasped. "Geez, Hallie, what are you doing? You don't know how to drive a gearshift! You could get a ticket!"

Hallie began to laugh hysterically.

Behind them, a red glow lit up the sky.

The town of Holyoake had just become its own burnt sacrifice.